FINN
AND THE
TIME-TRAVELING
PAJAMAS

FINN
AND THE
TIME-TRAVELING
PAJAMAS

MICHAEL BUCKLEY

DELACORTE PRESS

Text copyright © 2021 by Michael Buckley
Jacket art copyright © 2021 by Petur Antonsson

All rights reserved. Published in the United States by Delacorte Press,
an imprint of Random House Children's Books,
a division of Penguin Random House LLC, New York.

Delacorte Press is a registered trademark and the colophon is a trademark
of Penguin Random House LLC.

Visit us on the Web! rhcbooks.com

Educators and librarians, for a variety of teaching tools, visit us
at RHTeachersLibrarians.com

Library of Congress Cataloging-in-Publication Data
Names: Buckley, Michael, author.
Title: Finn and the time-traveling pajamas / Michael Buckley.
Description: First edition. | New York : Delacorte Press, [2021] | Series: Finn and
the intergalactic lunchbox ; book 2 | Audience: Ages 10 and up. | Summary: After
sixty years of trying to stop Paradox and set the universe right again, Finn time-
travels to get help from his nine-year-old self.
Identifiers: LCCN 2019056504 (print) | LCCN 2019056505 (ebook) |
ISBN 978-0-525-64691-4 (hardcover) | ISBN 978-0-525-64693-8 (library binding) |
ISBN 978-0-525-64692-1 (ebook)
Subjects: CYAC: Adventure and adventurers—Fiction. | Monsters—Fiction. |
Time travel—Fiction. | Science fiction.
Classification: LCC PZ7.B882323 Fit 2021 (print) | LCC PZ7.B882323 (ebook) |
DDC [Fic]—dc23

The text of this book is set in 11.25-point New Century Schoolbook LT Pro.

Printed in Canada
10 9 8 7 6 5 4 3 2 1
First Edition

*For
Shay Kileen*

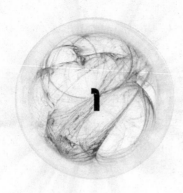

1

COLD SPRING, NY
60 YEARS IN THE FUTURE

Finn watched his friend Lincoln reach into the bag of goodies. That was what they called the collection of technologies they'd stolen from the future. Finn had lost track of what was inside it long ago. All he knew was that when Lincoln took something out of the bag, a huge explosion usually followed. This time he found a shiny silver ball covered in colored lights. It looked a lot like a Christmas ornament, only with a glass screen and a big red button on the side.

"All right, let's go over the plan one more time," Lincoln said. "This is a mini black hole emitter, compliments of the fine people of the thirtieth century. Now, before you push the button—"

There was a beep, and a red number ten glowed in the window. Then it became a nine. Then an eight.

"Did you push the button, Foley?" Lincoln asked.

"I did," Finn admitted. "I couldn't help myself. There was a button, and it was red!"

The window glowed with a number five.

"Did I tell you to push the button?" Lincoln yelled.

"No."

"Aaargh! Throw it! Now!"

Finn hefted the silver sphere as far as his old, wrinkled arm would allow. It arched into the sky, down the street, and toward a raging fire. Inside the flames stood a monster, roaring and tossing cars aside with its bare hands. It called itself Paradox, and today Finn and Lincoln were going to kill it. At least, that was the plan.

"What are you looking at, old man? Run!" Lincoln shouted and they took off at a sprint in the opposite direction. They weren't kids anymore. Both Finn and Lincoln were over seventy years old now, and the past sixty of them had mostly been filled with fighting, running, and explosions. All of it had taken its toll on their bodies. Finn's hip screamed in protest with every step. The rusty hinge on Lincoln's mechanical leg kept seizing and slowing him down, too. Still, they ran.

The sphere hit the ground with a massive *boom!* A

shock wave followed and knocked the men off their feet. As they tried to stand, Finn saw a swirling black void open where the sphere had landed. From it came an intense gravitational pull that sucked in everything that wasn't nailed down: lumber, porcelain tiles, busted appliances, old bicycles, trees, houses, everything was devoured by the hungry black emptiness. With the wind screaming in their ears, Finn and Lincoln dove behind an abandoned pickup truck, hoping it was heavy enough to avoid the pull. For a few moments it seemed as if they had made the right decision, but then the truck jerked forward, caught in the black hole's grip. Inch by inch it slid down the street. The men found themselves dragged toward oblivion.

"I don't suppose that thing has an off button!" Finn shouted over the chaos.

"No! It doesn't! If we get crushed to death inside a black hole, I will never forgive you!" Lincoln cried.

The pickup's front bumper kissed the surface of the void, and in a flash, the whole truck was gone. With nothing between them and certain death, Finn and Lincoln clawed at the bricks in the cobblestone street, fighting for their lives with only the strength in their fingertips. When it felt like they couldn't hold on any longer, the hungry void suddenly collapsed in on itself and disappeared. A calm came to the world around them.

"We're getting too old for this, derp," Lincoln grumbled.

"I haven't heard you call me that in a while," Finn said.

"Do you miss it?"

"Not so much," Finn replied, though he was glad his friend still had a sense of humor despite their situation. The truth was, they weren't *getting* too old—they were way past too old. He and Lincoln were both tired and gray. They should have been retired and living out their golden years on a beach in Florida. But here they were, still trying to save the world.

"Do you think it worked?" Lincoln said as he fiddled with his hinge. "Do you see Ugly anywhere?"

Finn scanned the neighborhood for the monster, his eyes burning from the smoke and heat. There was no sign of Paradox anywhere. Could he trust what he was seeing? Had they actually managed to kill Paradox?

"Is that cannon thing ready?" he asked. "Just in case it survived."

Lincoln shrugged. "I think so."

"What do you mean, you *think* so?"

"Well, it was in perfect working condition until you dropped it!"

"Are you seriously still mad about that? Future people were firing laser guns at us," Finn cried.

"Future people don't like it when you steal their stuff!" Lincoln grumbled.

Rustling in the debris brought the argument to a stop. Without another word, Lincoln reached into his bag and took out a long silver weapon. He placed it in Finn's hands.

"Put an end to this, Foley," Lincoln said. "If you kill it, everything can go back to the way it was supposed to be. No more running. No more scavenging for food, and no more magic jammies."

Finn looked down at himself. He was wearing a pair of pajamas decorated with cowboys swinging lassos and tumbleweeds. Some wore ten-gallon hats, others sheriff's badges, and all of them shared the same dopey smile. The pajamas were the only clothing he had worn in sixty years, and not a day had passed when he hadn't wished he could take them off.

"We'll get her back, too," Lincoln continued.

Julep.

Her face flashed in his memory. Despite all the years that had passed, losing Julep still hurt as badly as it had the day she died. He tried not to think of her anymore, but some nights she crept into his dreams, pushing her glasses up on her nose and carrying around her backpack full of weird books. She'd say something in her thick Southern accent and the voice sounded so real he'd wake up, wondering if somehow she had come back to them. Killing Paradox might bring her back to them, for real.

He hefted the cannon onto his shoulder and pressed his thumb against the firing button.

An explosion in the debris sent nails and glass and shingles flying in every direction. From the smoke rose a crackling ball of flames. It hovered in the sky over the men, staring down at them like a bloodshot eye, and inside it was the black outline of Paradox.

"Finn Foley!" Its voice sounded like a terrible accident, a rockslide crashing down on a busy highway, but it wasn't nearly as horrible as its owner. When the flames went out and the ball vanished, Paradox dropped to the ground, landing as nimbly as a cat. Finn fought back a scream. Paradox never failed to chill his blood. Its body was grotesque, stringy and long, covered in a hard black shell that cracked and splintered whenever it moved. The face was flat and featureless—no eyes, no nose, no mouth. Long, spiky hair stuck straight up from its head, each tip sparking with blue electricity.

"I am Paradox. I am the fixer, the reshaper of time and space. I am inevitable, and I have much work to do, but you deny me my destiny. For sixty years you have kept your secret, and for sixty years I have made you suffer. Why waste what little time you have left on this pointless fight? My destiny is to break this world in half and rebuild it into something better. He must be by my side. He must see that his efforts to destroy me were in vain. Tell me where he is!"

"Not this again," Lincoln said.

"Yeah, we've heard this speech like a million times. 'I am Paradox. I'm the big bad. I will destroy everything and rebuild it in my glorious vision.' Blah, blah, blah," Finn said.

"You mock me."

"Yes, consider yourself mocked," Finn said. He aimed the cannon at Paradox.

"More of your silly toys?" Paradox said. "You should know by now that you cannot kill me."

"Then it shouldn't bother you if we try." Finn pressed the firing button and a loud whirring filled the air. It was followed by a blast of heat and light and noise that slammed into the monster's chest. For the first time in sixty years, Paradox let loose a howl. The black armor that wrapped around its body was stripped away strand by strand, and the monster fell to its knees.

"You're hurting it. Don't stop!" Lincoln shouted.

"There's no chance of that, old friend," Finn cried.

And then, without warning, the engine inside the cannon let out a pop, followed by a whiff of smoke, and died.

"Don't say it, Lincoln!" Finn cried. He pounded on the side of the cannon, hoping to get it working again, but nothing helped.

"Don't say what? You mean don't say anything about how you dropped a super weapon from the year 2617 that was the first thing we've used that actually hurt the monster we've been trying to kill for sixty years? Is that what I'm not supposed to say?"

Paradox crawled to its feet, and in a sudden burst of speed, the creature snatched Finn's wrist, causing him to drop the cannon. The monster's grasp was super-human and the pain was unbearable. In the old days, Finn might have been able to pull himself free, but time had made him slow and weak.

Lincoln charged forward and threw his best right hook. The creature ducked and the punch never landed. With its free hand, Paradox wrapped its fingers around Lincoln's neck and squeezed.

"You are forcing me to do something I would rather not do. I'm going to give you one more chance, Finn Foley. Tell me where he is," it said.

"Kill me if you want, Ugly. I'm never going to tell you."

"I have no intention of killing you, Mr. Foley," Paradox said. A crackle of electricity swam down its arm into its fingertips, and then into Lincoln. The old man's body jerked. He let out a cry and then flew backward. Lincoln crashed against a fence. And didn't move again.

"Nooooo!" Finn bellowed.

"Oh, look at your face. Look at the anger! You have wasted your whole life. Everyone you have ever cared about is gone. You must think you have nothing left to lose now, but you're wrong. We're just getting started! I will go back to every happy moment of your life and demolish it. I will kill every person you ever knew, then go back and make sure I can kill them all over again. Time doesn't have me on a leash, Finn Foley. I can go anywhere. I can do anything. Tell me where he is. Where is your father? Where is Asher Foley?"

Finn fell to his knees, defeated and broken. Paradox was right. He had failed. He looked down at his shaking, wrinkled hands. Why was he still fighting? Maybe the monster was right? Maybe now was the time to bring it all to an end. If he told Paradox the truth, the pain would finally stop.

"This is over, Finn Foley," Paradox continued. "You were never going to win. You can't stop destiny. Put away your cowboy pajamas. You put up a good fight. Your dad would be proud. Now tell me where he is."

Wait. Cowboy pajamas.

"This is far from over, Ugly," Finn said, then closed his eyes. *Please,* he silently begged—not to Paradox, but to Time itself. After decades jumping through it, he'd come to believe it listened to him. Sometimes it seemed to make things easy. Other times it could be fickle. Now he needed to go someplace outside of time and space. He needed to go to a place he'd promised he'd never visit again. *Are you listening?*

"Pajamas, take me to the Ranch," he shouted.

He braced for rejection, but then his hair stood on end. He felt the familiar sparks in his fingertips and watched the big golden bubble surround him in its protective shield.

"Thank you!" he cried.

"NO!" Paradox pounded on the bubble's skin, but its attack did no harm.

"I'll see you very soon," Finn promised, and then the bubble sank into the ground. There was a flash of light, and he found himself in a tube of neon energy. He realized what he was doing was crazy—going to the Ranch was maybe the worst idea he'd ever had. But there he would find the one person in the universe who could help him stop the monster for good, and save everyone he had ever loved.

Himself.

2

COLD SPRING, NY
PRESENT DAY

Finn Foley lay in his backyard admiring the creamy blue sky. The sun was bright and warm, but a breeze coming off Bear Mountain made everything nice and comfy. Honeybees buzzed in the flower bed near the back door, and somewhere a happy dog was barking. Lincoln Sidana and Julep Li, his two best friends, were lying in the grass next to him. It was as perfect a summer day as the world had ever seen.

"I'm dying of boredom," Lincoln groaned.

"I can't take it anymore," Finn said.

"Saving the world ruined us," Julep complained.

It was true. Six months ago, Finn and his friends

had defeated an alien invasion. In the process, they'd visited strange planets and hung out with a glitchy robot and a lady with too many eyeballs. Now the world was safe. Everything that used to excite them was now flat and dull.

Video games seemed painfully slow. Exploring the woods was tedious. Even their weekly cannonball competitions in Lincoln's pool couldn't hold back the yawns.

"Let's do something," Finn said, "before I go insane."

"I've got an idea." Julep sat up and opened her backpack. She pulled out her collection of books on unusual topics—everything from fighting off evil curses to the Loch Ness Monster. Julep carried them everywhere she went.

The boys shared a knowing look. Julep's "ideas" usually involved traipsing through the woods searching for missing links and vampires, and risking Lyme disease. Finn humored her "research," mainly because . . . well, he didn't want to call it a crush, exactly. It was more a feeling of being happy and barfy at the same time. All he would admit to himself was that he liked having her around.

"Hard pass if it involves Bigfoot," Lincoln muttered.

"C'mon!" Julep said.

"I can't spend another minute in the woods looking for something that doesn't exist. I just got over the worst case of poison ivy my doctor has ever seen," Lincoln explained.

Julep turned to Finn for support. He cringed.

"Maybe we could do something that doesn't turn us into lunch for a million hungry mosquitos?" he said.

Julep scrunched up her face and shoved her books back in her pack.

"You guys suck. There are tons of documented sightings of Bigfoot in the Hudson Valley. She is in those hills waiting to be discovered."

"'She'? I thought Bigfoot was a dude," Lincoln said.

"You would," she huffed. "You'll regret it when some other kid gets the first picture of her!"

"Even if you find Lady Bigfoot, the men in the sunglasses will take your phone, just like the last time," Lincoln said.

Julep growled. After the kids had stopped the Plague from conquering the world, men from a secret government agency combed every inch of Finn's neighborhood, confiscating everything alien, including all the pictures on Julep's phone. Her trip to the planet Nemeth, Highbeam and his twenty-five robot kids, even Dax Dargon and her blue skin were now just memories. The spaceship in the sky was explained away as a big-budget science-fiction movie shoot. Everyone in the neighborhood was told to keep their mouth shut about what really happened, or they would disappear just like Julep's pictures. Finn sympathized with her. Julep was passionate about uncovering the truth. She believed in things most people didn't, and because of that, kids at school avoided her. For a brief moment, she'd had proof that she wasn't a weirdo. Now all she had of their amazing experiences was a bunch of stories she wasn't allowed to tell.

Without warning, a bright and dazzling light appeared. It was like a second sun had decided to rise in Finn's backyard. It spun like a top in midair, a perfect circle with flames for edges. Then *WHOOSH!* From the center stepped one of the strangest creatures Finn had ever seen. He was tall and lean with skin the color of a shiny penny, but that was where the easy descriptions ended. First, he didn't have a nose but sported a long gray mustache that hung like a pair of upside-down handlebars on a bike. Steel bands were implanted on either side of his skull, and they crackled with blue sparks, but by far the weirdest thing was his clothes. He looked like he had stepped out of an old cowboy movie—jeans, leather chaps, boots with spurs, a red handkerchief tied around his neck, and a tall white ten-gallon hat. A silver star was pinned to his chest, engraved with an hourglass, and he twirled a lasso that seemed to be generating the portal. When the rope stopped spinning, the doorway disappeared.

He stuck a long finger in his mouth, then raised it into the air and caught the breeze. "Right year, right backyard. All right, y'all come with me," he said.

"Um, no?" Lincoln said.

The strange cowboy squinted at the kids.

"My name is Zeke. I work for the Time Rangers," he said.

"Good for you," Finn said.

Zeke sighed impatiently. "The Time Rangers who protect the past, present, and future?"

Julep immediately reached for her phone and snapped a picture of him.

"You ain't heard of us?" he continued.

"No offense, but we've met a lot of aliens. The excitement has kind of worn off," Finn said. "So what exactly do you want?"

"You have to meet with the other Rangers. They want to talk to you, pronto!"

"Um, yeah, we're gonna pass. You know, the whole stranger danger thing," Lincoln said.

Sparks shot out of the implants on Zeke's temples.

"He didn't tell you anything about us?" the cowboy asked Finn.

"Who?"

"Your dad," Zeke said. "Asher Foley."

Finn felt like he had been smacked in the back of the head.

"What did you say? You know my dad?" he asked.

"Yes. Now, you come on. Time's a-wastin'," Zeke said. He twirled his lasso faster and faster, until the rope caught fire and a new, shimmering portal appeared inside it.

"He really thinks we're going with him, doesn't he?" Julep asked.

"Go back to your space rodeo," Lincoln said. "Before we call the cops!"

"What do you know about my dad?" Finn asked.

"Come with me and I will tell you everything," Zeke replied.

Finn got to his feet.

"Really? You're going to run off with an alien 'cause he says he knows your dad?" Lincoln asked. "Fine. Go! I'll tell your mom you were a moron. I think she knows already."

"I have to know," Finn said.

"Finn, Lincoln is right," Julep said. "You can't go alone."

"Enough yammerin'," Zeke said, and with a flick of his wrist, the lasso twirled over the kids.

There was a blinding light, but Finn didn't need his eyes to know he wasn't in his backyard anymore. The cool and quiet breeze was replaced by sweltering heat and the sounds of sawing and hammering and . . . Wait! Was that a cow mooing? When his eyes finally adjusted, he found they were standing in a wide, grassy field bordered by a split-rail fence. A rustic ranch house with a porch stood a few yards away, a chimney rising from the roof. A two-story barn painted bright red sat next to it. Horses and goats milled in and out of its wide-open doors, and chickens ran freely around the property. An angry rooster squawked at a lazy goat that munched on grass it pulled from the ground with its teeth. It was like a country song come to life, except for the collection of weirdos rushing around, fixing things, patching the ranch's roof, and painting the barn. Like Zeke, they wore cowboy outfits, but otherwise none of them resembled him, and they weren't any more human than he was. One had a television set for a head; another looked like a walking beanbag. There was one who resembled a peacock with human legs, and still another that looked like a huge yellow raincoat come to life. Working on the barn was a cyclops that stood nearly fifteen feet tall.

"Welcome to the Ranch," Zeke said.

"And that is what, exactly?" Julep said as she took more pictures with her phone.

"Think of it as the heart of the space-time continuum. All of time moves through this stretch of land, though it don't usually look this bad. We had a time twister spin through here a few days back. Tore the place up something good. For a little while you couldn't tell yesterday from tomorrow, or today from next year, but we're slowly making repairs."

"Little good it's gonna do us. Looks like another storm is headed our way," the beanbag groused with a nod to the sky.

Finn turned his eyes to the east. Black clouds were gathering there.

"The Rangers are set to do something about that today, Gus," Zeke promised.

The beanbag harrumphed and went back to work.

"That lasso brought us here?" Julep asked. "How does it work?"

"Trade secret, young lady," Zeke said.

Finn could almost see the questions piling up inside Julep's head, but before she could ask another, someone shouted a warning. Two green blobs with faces pushed a wheelbarrow full of bricks directly into their path, and the group was forced to jump out of the way or get run over.

"Sorry!" the blobs called in unison.

"C'mon. The others are waiting." Zeke led the children onto the porch of the ranch house. He kicked a post to get the dust off his boots, causing his spurs to jingle; then he spit something brown into the dirt. As he reached for the door, a strange lady charged through. Her body was like an enormous carrot, with orange skin and a stalk of green hair to match. Her faded dress stopped at her ankles, and she wore an apron wrapped tightly around her waist. She carried a steel pot under her arm.

"Mornin', Zeke," she said.

"Mornin', Cookie."

"Are these the kids?"

"Yes, ma'am," Zeke said.

"Keep 'em out of my kitchen," the woman demanded. "They've caused enough of a ruckus around here."

"Will do, Cookie."

The carrot lady gave the kids a disgusted look, then waddled toward the barn with her pot.

"What was that about?" Finn said. "What ruckus have we caused?"

Again, Zeke ignored their questions and hurried everyone inside the house. There they found a room with wide plank floors filled with worn antique furniture. A player piano rested against a wall tinkling out an old song. A rifle hung above the fireplace mantel, and a couple of oil lamps bathed everything in a flickering golden glow. Bizarre animal heads were mounted on the walls. One looked like a cross between a panda and a wild boar. Another was an overgrown duck, but instead of feathers it had thick, matted fur in strange colors. At the far end of the room was a set of double doors with shining brass handles. A plaque was mounted on each with the same hourglass design as the one on Zeke's badge.

"Now, listen up," Zeke said. "Miss Ellie has no patience for shenanigans. If you're smart, you will keep the lip-flapping to a minimum. Best let me do the talking."

"Who is Miss Ellie?" Lincoln asked.

"And what does this have to do with my dad?" Finn demanded.

Zeke waved them off and pushed the trio through the doors. One step inside and every question they had was replaced with a new one. The room beyond baffled their brains. To begin with, the word *room* didn't seem like the right way to describe the space. It was round, and instead of walls and a ceiling there was a dense, ghostly smoke. Floating inside it were little movies, moments of people's lives from all over the world. They were framed by flames, and each burned to ash and fell to the floor after only a few moments. Once they were gone, more appeared to take their place.

Finn was mesmerized as he watched the people in the movies talk and work and live their lives, all seemingly unaware they were being watched. An old woman and a little girl made cookies from scratch. A man stood on a dock and wept after throwing a bouquet of flowers into the water. Two kids ran through a forest, laughing and holding hands. A woman got down on one knee and proposed to her girlfriend. A pretty blond lady whispered "I love you" to the sleeping man beside her. Each moment was deeply personal, and though Finn felt guilty for spying, he couldn't look away.

"What is this?" Julep asked.

"We call it the Campfire," Zeke explained. "There are a zillion stories inside it that need to stay on track. We watch them to make sure they do."

"So you spy on people. Creepy," Lincoln said.

"It ain't spying!" Zeke snapped. "There are some ornery cusses in this universe. I'm talking about chrono rustlers and hour smugglers and eon bandits. If we don't keep an eye out for them, they'll make a mess of things."

"That guy washing his car is dangerous?" Julep asked, pointing to one of the movies just as it turned to ash.

"Of course not. Normally, the Campfire would focus on the real troublemakers, but the twister made a mess of things and it hasn't worked right since. For now, it's all Earth all the time, which is not ideal. Most of the criminals are on the more advanced worlds. In fact, you three are one of the first humans to ever give us a headache."

"Us?" Lincoln said.

The double doors opened again, and eleven unusual

creatures stepped into the room. Each was dressed like Zeke, with boots and hats and bandannas, but none of them looked like the strange copper man. There was a creature with a groundhog's head, a boxy robot with dangly arms, a dark-skinned woman with bleached white hair who wore two glowing revolvers strapped to her waist, something that looked like a walking egg, a wolf as large as a rhino, a translucent blob that left a trail of slime behind it, and a handful of other beings just as unique. Each took off their hat, kicked dust off their boots, and sat down in one of the massive chairs.

"This is nuts." Lincoln laughed. "There's a giant egg over there wearing a bandanna."

"Show some respect," Zeke scolded. "Her name is Pearl, and like all Time Rangers, she was chosen to defend the continuum. Ours is a sacred duty and an honor."

"I hope I didn't insult her," Lincoln snarked. "I wouldn't want her to get scrambled. Or is she more the hard-boiled type? If she wants to fight, I'm getting the shell out of here."

Finn and Julep couldn't help but laugh.

Zeke pressed his hands against the steel bands on his temples. It seemed to calm him.

"Shhh! Miss Ellie is about to speak."

Miss Ellie's chaps were made from reptile skins and teeth. Her long snow-white hair was tied into a braid that hung to her feet. Her revolvers pulsated as if mimicking the rhythm of her heartbeat.

"Attention, Time Rangers," she said, and everyone grew quiet. "Zeke has gone to Earth and retrieved Finn Foley, Lincoln Sidana, and Julep Li. They are ready to defend themselves. Zeke are you ready?"

"Yes, ma'am."

"Very good," Miss Ellie said. "Buford, let's get started."

The clunky robot got up from his seat and stood in the center of the room. His body looked like a collection of ancient electronics someone had set out on the curb on trash day. Every time he moved, he produced a honk, a crash, or a grinding sound. He cleared his throat, and his eyes projected a holographic document for everyone to see.

"I will read the accusations. These children—"

"Accusations?" Julep repeated, her voice rising.

"What is this?" Finn demanded.

The cowboy pulled the children into a huddle.

"This is a trial. I'm going to do my best to get you out of trouble, but if you keep interrupting, Miss Ellie will lose her patience, and you really, really don't want that to happen. Now, please. Let me do my job!" Zeke turned back to the Time Rangers. "Sorry for the interruption."

"As I was saying, these children are accused of crimes against time, including the creation of a Class

Three time twister, damage to the Ranch, altering history and the future, theft of advanced technologies, possession of an unauthorized time machine, creation of a new life-form—"

"Do you understand what he's saying?" Finn whispered to Julep.

She shook her head.

"—and splintering a timeline."

"Thank you, Buford. You may argue your case," Miss Ellie said. Her face grew dark and angry, while her revolvers glowed white-hot. "But let no one be mistaken. Children or not, if they are found guilty, the punishment will be severe."

3

Finn didn't understand much of what Miss Ellie said, but he knew what she meant—they were in big trouble. This trip was not about his father at all. Zeke lured them to this stupid trial with lies. The betrayal left a bitter taste in his mouth, but he held his tongue, wondering where all this might go.

"The children plead not guilty," Zeke said to a chorus of boos.

"Is anyone surprised?" the groundhog man barked. "Zeke never allows his clients to plead guilty."

"Silence!" Miss Ellie shouted. Her voice was like thunder. The crowd stopped their complaining. A few looked shaken by her anger.

"My clients cannot confess to crimes they haven't committed," Zeke shouted.

"What is it you think we did?" Lincoln demanded.

"You went back in time and changed the future," Buford said.

"Whoa! Whoa! Whoa! Whoa! Whoa! I know a lot about time travel, and if we'd done that, I would be the first to know!" Julep cried.

"Then I'll show you," Buford said.

Finn watched the robot tap his silver star, and one of the movies floated out of the smoke. In it, he saw Lincoln, Julep, and himself sitting in his backyard. A bright pink unicorn lunchbox was resting in the grass next to them.

"Six months ago, you came into possession of an alien technology that opened wormholes to other worlds. It drew the attention of a race of intelligent insects known as the Plague. With an invasion looming over your planet, you used the machine to find your long-lost father so that you could say goodbye. But Asher Foley was not in your timeline. He was in the past. So the wormhole machine broke through the time barrier and took you and your friends to his last known appearance—August 16, 2018."

Finn remembered that day in his backyard very well, and he remembered the wormhole. It hadn't been like any of the whirlpools before it. This one locked him inside a shimmering golden bubble and delivered him to the backyard of his old house in Garrison, New York, the one he'd lived in before his dad walked out on the family.

"So it's true?" Lincoln asked. "We went back in time?"

"Yes, it's true," Zeke said, then turned to the others. "We ain't arguing that it happened. We're saying it was an accident. Look at 'em. These kids aren't smart enough to know what they did. They're basically morons."

"Hey!" Julep frowned.

"An accident, he says!" Buford shook his metal fist in the air. "When you nearly break every rule of time travel, it's hardly an accident."

"There are rules of time travel?" Julep asked.

The Time Rangers stood and in unison they recited the rules.

"Rule number one: Don't time travel. Rule number two: If you do time travel, don't change anything about the past or the future. Rule number three: Avoid encounters with versions of yourself, and never ever, ever make physical contact with them."

"These delinquents broke all three!" Buford roared. "They time traveled, they changed the past and the future, and Finn had a face-to-face conversation with a future version of himself. If they had accidentally touched one another all of existence would have unraveled. Bingo! Bango! Kaput!"

Zeke sighed and tapped his silver star. The first movie burned away, and a new one floated over to take its place. In it, a scruffy old man wore a pair of pajamas.

"Hey! That's the guy we saw wandering around in my backyard," Finn said, recalling the cranky stranger they'd met when he and his friends had supposedly gone back in time.

"That's not some old dude, Finn Foley. That's you, sixty years in the future," Zeke explained.

"Me?" Finn cried. When he studied the old man's face, he gasped. Zeke wasn't lying. It really was him! He had the same eyes, the same ears—he even had the same grin! But how was it possible? Time travel was the stuff of movies and comic books, not real life.

"Yes, you!" said Miss Ellie. "And you're easily the most dangerous criminal we've ever come up against, except maybe Paradox."

"I don't get it. How does talking to an older version of himself wreck the future?" Julep asked.

"The old man gave you the secret to kicking the tar out of the Plague," the robot explained.

"Huh?" Finn said.

"Unicorns, Finn. Your sister wanted you to ask the unicorns for help. In the original timeline, you told her she was being silly, but in the new timeline, Old Finn encouraged you to listen to her ideas. It saved Earth, which was not supposed to happen."

"Personally, I think we can all agree the change was for the better," Zeke said.

"It is not our decision to make, Zeke," Miss Ellie said. "Time Rangers do not pick winners and losers. We do not interfere with history's path. It is a violation of the vow you made when you joined us. Finn's decision to recruit the unicorns rewrote everything, which is why the Ranch was nearly destroyed by time twisters and the Campfire is all but useless to us. It's also why we now have two Finn Foleys wreaking havoc everywhere they go!"

"The old man's advice did more than change the future. It splintered the timeline!" Buford said.

Julep stepped forward and raised her hand as if she were in a classroom. "It seems to me there is an easy way to fix this," she said. "Just tell us all the things Old Man Finn has done, and together we'll make sure our Finn doesn't do them."

"Unfortunately, that's no longer an option." Zeke tapped his silver star. The new movie that appeared contained nothing but a horizontal line moving across the screen to the right. "This line represents Finn's lifetime. It's supposed to move forward and never change, unless . . ."

Suddenly, the line forked and became two lines running parallel to one another.

". . . he had a face-to-face meeting with his future.

When that happens, it's kind of like giving Time a punch in the belly. It can't make sense of two Finns, so to make things right it breaks them apart, turning them into completely separate people. Now nothing you do will affect Old Man Finn. Your choices will make no impact on his life at all. Even if you died, the old version of you would continue to live. It's called a splinter."

"And it's darn near impossible to fix! If you ask me, the old man did it on purpose so we couldn't use the boy to fix his mess!" Buford shouted. "I'm sure he thinks they're pretty funny. The man is a menace! Just look at him!"

Buford pressed the silver star on his chest. All the movies turned to ash and a new one appeared. Unlike the others, this wasn't a memory or a chart to explain time splinters; it was a collection of moments: Finn and his friends shooting laser guns, jumping through fires, stealing flying motorcycles, and popping up in different locations, all while fighting a hideous pitch-black monster.

"But all the chaos and stealing and nonsense are not nearly the biggest problem. It's Paradox. The monster is the worst thing we've ever faced. It's determined to destroy Time itself. Old Man Finn and his friends created it—"

"That was an accident!" Zeke shouted.

"Maybe so, but who's to say this Finn, the younger

one, won't accidentally create another? We can't take that risk!" the robot cried.

"With a little supervision I know I can keep that from happening. I have already taken steps to prevent more trouble. I followed them to the past and sabotaged their wormhole device so that it self-destructed."

"Hey! That nearly killed me," Finn shouted.

"They no longer have the ability to alter history and pose no further threat to the continuum. The right thing to do is cut them loose and send them home."

"I believe we have heard enough. It is time to vote," Miss Ellie said.

"Wait! There's one more thing. Finn is Asher Foley's son," Zeke said.

The Time Rangers went quiet. Finn could see they were conflicted. It was obvious they knew his dad, but how? And why?

"Asher should have taught his son the rules," Miss Ellie said. "Buford, what do you think is the appropriate punishment for Finn and his friends?"

"I recommend they be sent to the Barn," Buford said.

"The Barn? Buford, that's outrageous!" Zeke said hotly.

Miss Ellie locked her cold eyes on Finn as if she were searching for something good inside him.

"Zeke argues that Finn Foley, Julep Li, and Lincoln Sidana pose no threat to the continuum and therefore should be returned to their timelines, unpunished. If you agree, raise your hand, or the closest thing you have to one."

Aside from himself, Lincoln, and Julep, the only one who raised a hand was Zeke. The vote enraged the copper alien, and the steel implants on his head sparked with angry electricity.

"Shame on all of you!" he shouted at the others.

"The verdict is decided," Miss Ellie said. "Finn Foley and his friends are guilty of crimes against Time. Take them to the Barn."

4

Four hulking creatures with gray skin and rhino horns charged into the room. They wore boots and denim overalls, like they were farmhands. Before Finn could put up a fight, they dragged him and his friends outside.

"What are you going to do to us?" Julep shouted. The rhino men ignored her, but Zeke followed closely, demanding the children be treated with respect.

The guards swung the barn doors open and the smell of livestock invaded Finn's nose. Inside was an old tractor, bales of hay, and various farming tools, but nothing else in the Barn made sense. First, the inside was much bigger than the outside. The ceiling was impossibly high, with rows and rows of haylofts that went so high that Finn couldn't see where they stopped. On each level were wooden stalls, but instead of housing a horse or a donkey, they contained a unique and wildly unusual being. The group's arrival caused a frenzy of shouting and angry threats. Fists, flippers, and feathers slammed heavily against invisible walls that shimmered with each impact.

"Look! Is that Pre'at?" Lincoln pointed to the floor directly above them. Inside one of the cells was a sweaty, pale Alcherian. She looked like their scientist friend, except for all the unfriendly eyes.

While Julep and Lincoln marveled, Finn started to understand what the Barn was all about.

"This is a prison," he said.

"Yes. We house the worst of the worst: bandits, thieves, smugglers, killers-for-hire," Zeke explained. "The Rangers give everyone a chance to change their ways, but some are a bit too stubborn. We lock 'em up until they can be trusted."

"How long does that take?" Finn asked as he eyed a scaly yellow alien make a gesture as if he were breaking a branch in half.

"Hard to say. Some of them have been waiting a good long time. We got a handful that have been here ten thousand years."

"Ten thousand years! That's not possible," Julep cried.

"It is if you don't get old. Time works a bit differently

here on the Ranch," Zeke said, then turned to Finn. "Listen, I know the three of you don't belong in here. You're being punished for crimes you will never commit, but I have an idea. If I can find and capture the Old Man Finn, I might be able to get you out of here. That's who the Rangers really want. So for now, the best thing you three can do is sit tight and not cause a ruckus."

"Sit tight for how long? Ten thousand years? I should never have listened to you! You lied to me! You said this was about my dad!" Finn cried.

"Simmer down, cowpoke. This is about your dad," Zeke said. "All of this mess is about Asher Foley. Son, he didn't abandon your family. He was kidnapped."

"Kidnapped? Who would kidnap my dad?"

"You," Zeke said.

"Stop talking to me like I'm a moron."

"Kid, I don't mean you. I mean the other you. Old Man Finn got there just before you did. He came up behind your dad and put some kind of device on him. A second later, *poof!* He was gone. I've watched it in the Campfire a million times. It doesn't make any sense. Somehow your dad just vanished from the timeline. That's not supposed to be possible."

"But why would he do that? Why would Old Finn kidnap his own father?" Julep asked.

"He's trying to protect him from Paradox," Zeke said. "It wants to destroy the universe, and for some reason it needs Asher to do it. That's why Old Man Finn has spent the last sixty years of his life trying to stop that monster, and causing mayhem everywhere he goes."

Finn felt like he was drowning in questions. There were too many twists happening at once—time travelers dressed as cowboys, a barn full of alien criminals, and now this—*Dad didn't walk out on the family. I hid him from a monster.* Every day of anger, heartache, insecurity, and bitterness Finn ever felt and blamed on his dad was his own fault.

Cookie waddled into the Barn pushing a wheelbarrow. Her big pot was sitting inside it, and there was something moving around under the lid.

"Getting windy out there, Zeke. That sky is worrisome. Best get this done as fast as we can. Are they ready?"

"I haven't had a chance to explain this part," Zeke confessed.

Cookie spat on the ground.

"Well, tell 'em, and make sure they know not to give me any trouble," the carrot woman said. She reached into her apron pocket and took out a long silver ladle, then removed the pot's lid. Inside were three silver globs floating in hot water. She dipped the ladle into the soup and pulled one of them out.

"Kids, Cookie is here to make your dupes," Zeke said.

"Our what?" Lincoln asked.

"Clones, I guess is a better way to say it," Zeke said.

Before Finn could stop her, Cookie dumped the silver glob into his hands. Finn's first instinct was to drop it, but a comforting tingle raced from his fingertips all the way to the base of his spine. It felt silky and warm, and suddenly, all his anger and frustration about being deceived melted away, replaced by something that made him both sleepy and happy at the same time, like a big, loving hug from his mom. The ranch hands seemed to notice, and let him go.

"Is this thing purring?" Finn asked as he peered at his glob. It sounded like a happy kitten.

"That's why we call 'em copycats," Cookie explained, ladling a glob into Julep's hands. Finn watched the disgust on his friend's face quickly fall away. A moment later, the rhino men let her go, too, and she held the goop up to her cheek and smiled.

"It's so cute!" she sang.

"What's it doing?" Finn's copycat crawled up his arm, along his shoulder, and onto his head. He had a faint idea that he should be alarmed, but the creature seemed so safe and loving.

"Now, it's going to use your brain like a scratching post," Cookie explained, "but it won't hurt. It's just digging into your personality and memories. Once it's seen what you are, it will turn itself into a perfect copy of you, only one that's a bit less troublesome. Just sit tight. It takes a few minutes."

"Take all the time you want. It's like I'm in a burrito made of love," Julep said as her copycat made its way to the top of her head.

"What are the copies for?" Lincoln demanded. Finn was surprised by his friend's anger. What was he mad about? Everything was comfy and cozy, like taking a swim in tapioca pudding.

"While you're here in the Barn, we need to make sure no one misses you back home, so we send the copies to take over your lives. They'll make sure you live the boring and eventless existence you were always meant to lead. No one will notice a difference." Cookie scooped up the last of the copycats and tried to pour it into Lincoln's open hands, but the boy backed away.

"Keep that thing away from me!" he shouted. "There's only one Lincoln Sidana, and it's staying that way."

"Zeke! Tell the boy to stop fussin'!" Cookie demanded. "It ruins the batch."

Lincoln refused to listen. With renewed strength, he fought the ranch hands and managed to squirm free.

"Lincoln, calm down!" Zeke said. "You're going to make this harder for everyone."

"Lincoln needs a hug," Julep said.

"I agree," Finn replied. "Dude, chillax. You're harshing our mellow."

Cookie crept up behind Lincoln and dropped the copycat directly on top of his head. The relaxing sensation Finn and Julep were enjoying didn't seem to apply to Lincoln. He thrashed around, knocking over Cookie's wheelbarrow and pulling the copycat off his skull. Lincoln flung it to the floor, where he gave it a heavy stomp. The copycat whimpered and slowly slithered into a corner.

"You two are morons," Lincoln growled as he charged across the room toward his friends. Before the rhino men could stop him, he yanked Julep's copycat off her head and drop-kicked it against the barn wall. By the surprised look on her face, Julep's calm, easy feeling was gone. Now she was red-faced and angry.

"Oh no you didn't!" she bellowed, and along with Lincoln she went after Finn's copycat. Julep hurled it into a corner, where it crashed with a watery splat. Like her, Finn's dreamy pleasantness was replaced by a rush of anger.

"Keep your slimy kittens away from us," Finn said.

"What in tarnation!" Cookie shouted. She retrieved one of the mushed globs and brushed away the hay and sawdust it collected. "This batch took me all morning to make, and you've ruined them. Uh-oh, look! They're transforming!"

The copycat in her hand swirled and churned like a tiny tornado. Cookie set it on the barn floor just before it doubled in size, then tripled. The other two copycats were doing the same thing, and soon each one was as tall as Finn. Their sparkly silver color morphed into a rainbow of hues, taking on the distinct skin tones of each kid. Hair sprouted. Teeth appeared. Even the freckles on Finn's nose and cheeks came forward. It was wearing the same clothes, had the same haircut, and even had the same bruise on his arm from falling out of a tree a few days prior. When the change was complete, the copycat looked exactly like him. Julep and Lincoln were facing duplicates of their own, too.

"Is this supposed to be me? I'm not that chubby," Lincoln grumbled.

Despite Lincoln's complaints, the clones were identical to them in every way, except for a few bizarre differences. For one, their eyes were spinning in their sockets. Second, drool slid out of the corners of their mouths. And finally, Lincoln's clone got down on his hands and knees and rubbed his head against the real Lincoln's leg, purring like a kitten. Julep's copy was just as bonkers. It roared with laughter, then ran face-first into a wall. The impact knocked her silly and she fell onto her back. A moment later, she giggled, got up, and did it all over again.

"They're defective," Cookie complained.

"You're telling me." Finn watched a long white tail slip through the back of his clone's pants.

"Can you fix 'em?" Zeke asked as he righted the wheelbarrow.

"No, I can't fix 'em! I have to reboot them and start from scratch. Miss Ellie is gonna be furious. She wanted them inserted into the timeline right away!" the woman said. She turned to the clones and did her best to get them to follow her out of the Barn.

"I don't care!" Finn shouted. "You basically kidnapped us and are planning to throw us in jail for ten thousand years, and now you want to replace us with these morons! I've met a lot of aliens, but you are the worst!"

"Uh-oh. Not now. This is the last thing I need," Zeke said.

The kids ignored him. There was a peculiar energy in the air, like a buildup of electricity, and it was getting stronger and stronger.

"Do you feel that?" Finn asked. His hair was standing on end. "What's happening?"

Outside, someone was ringing a bell.

"We got another twister on its way," the beanbag creature said when it popped into the Barn. "Better take cover."

"NO!" Zeke cried. "That's not just a twister!"

A huge golden globe appeared out of thin air. It came with an explosion that knocked everyone off their feet. When Finn recovered, he looked up and saw that there was a man inside it, but he couldn't make out his face. The bubble popped and the figure inside leaped forward and planted a knee in Zeke's belly. The alien's metallic implants came loose from his head and clanged onto the dirt floor. Without them, Zeke slumped to his knees, looking weak and barely conscious. While this was happening, the stranger continued with a flurry of fists. He attacked the ranch hands, punching one in the face and kicking another in the chest, sending both of them tumbling to the ground. The other two suffered vicious blows and were knocked unconscious within seconds. When the fight was over, the figure leaned forward to catch his breath and kept whispering "Thank you" into the air. Finn was finally able to focus on his hero. He was an elderly man with a mop of gray hair and a face full of wrinkles. He was also wearing cowboy pajamas.

"It's you!" Finn said. It was Old Man Finn!

"Lincoln was right. I am getting too old for this," the man said. He bent over one of the ranch hands and yanked a bizarre weapon off its belt. A second later, he shoved it into Lincoln's hands. "They call it a Chrono-Disrupter. The button is right here. Have fun."

"What are you doing here?" Finn asked.

"No questions. We don't have time. I need to give you something," the old man said. He stepped behind the tractor, and Finn heard him unbutton his pajamas. A moment later, the approaching storm hit the Ranch with shocking ferocity. The wind howled outside like an angry dog, and through the open barn doors Finn saw a horrible black-and-purple tornado cutting across the field toward them.

Old Man Finn didn't seem the least bit concerned. When he stepped out from behind the tractor, his pajamas were wadded up in his hands. Finn was grateful to see that he had clothes on underneath.

"Put these on," the old man said as he shoved the pajamas into the boy's hands.

"Huh? Why?"

"Just do it!"

Finn threw the pajamas on the floor and tried to snatch the old man by the wrist. He had questions that needed answers, but Old Finn pulled away in shock.

"Are you nuts? Don't you know the rules of time travel? No touching! Do you want everything to unravel?"

"I don't care about your stupid rules. Zeke told me you kidnapped my dad. Where is he?" Finn shouted.

"First, he's *our* dad!" Old Man Finn said. "Second,

he's safe and in a place where Paradox can't get him. Telling you more won't help anyone, but trust me, he's closer than you think."

"That's not good enough," Finn said. "Do you realize you ruined my life?"

Something banged against the outside of the Barn, startling the cows and horses. They lowed and whinnied with fear. The whole building felt like it might blow away. Two horses dashed into the Barn in a panic. They nearly knocked Lincoln and Julep down.

"Um, maybe we should find some shelter?" Lincoln said as he eyed the storm through an open window. Unfortunately, both Finns ignored him.

"I did what had to be done," the old man cried. "That's all I've ever done—not that it helped me much. Sixty years and I still can't stop Paradox. Well, kid, I've run out of time and ideas. You're the last trick I've got up my sleeve."

"Me?"

"You heard me. You're the twist in the story, kid— the one thing Paradox will never see coming. If it works, you can put everything back the way it was supposed to be—including our dad. But first you have to pick up the pajamas and put them on! Unless you and your buddies want to spend the next ten thousand years locked up in this Barn."

Finn looked down at the pajamas and snarled. This

was just one more weird event in a day full of weird-ness.

"If I do, will you tell me where you hid Dad?"

"I'll tell you after you help me stop Paradox," Old Man Finn promised.

Finn threw up his hands in surrender and snatched the pajamas off the ground. What choice did he have but to do as his older version told him? He did his best to step into them, buttoning himself up in the front. They were a little snug in all the worst places, but they fit. Lincoln's laughter was all he needed to know that he looked ridiculous.

"You are adorbs," Lincoln said. "I especially like the cowboys."

Julep's face was red with embarrassment for him.

"Happy?" he shouted at the old man. "Now what do you want me to do?"

"Trust me, I know better than anyone how ridicu-lous you look, but the pj's are probably the most ad-vanced machine ever invented. I've programmed them to take you to three specific dates."

"Programmed the pj's?" Lincoln asked. "What does that mean?"

"The pajamas are a time machine," the old man ex-plained.

"No way!" Julep cried.

There was shouting and whistling outside the Barn.

"They're sending more ranch hands. C'mon," Old Man Finn said. He hurried the kids to a ladder that led to the loft. It went higher and higher, seemingly forever. He ordered everyone to climb.

"Time-traveling pajamas?" Julep continued. "How do they work?"

"I couldn't tell you even if I knew. What's important is what you do with them. Go to the three dates I've preprogrammed. When you get to each one, you'll find yourself in the middle of my biggest fights with Paradox. I need you to do something unexpected, something that distracts the monster from the fight. Start a fire. Dress up like chickens. It doesn't matter. Just create some mischief. A distraction might be all I need to finally beat that ugly thing."

"Just so I understand," Lincoln called out as he climbed. "You want us to be time-traveling trouble-makers?"

"Is there anyone better for the job than Lincoln Sidana?" the old man asked. "Climb faster. They're coming!"

Finn glanced down and saw more of the horned ranch hands race into the Barn. When they spotted the group, they started climbing after them.

"Get off at the next level," Old Finn shouted.

Once there, the kids scampered off the ladder. Their

arrival launched the prisoners into a hostile frenzy. Old Man Finn told the kids to ignore it and led them through the rows of cells like he was maneuvering them through a maze.

"They're going to catch us," Lincoln said. "There's no exit."

"We're not trying to escape. We're just killing time," Old Man Finn said as he eyed his wristwatch. "The pajamas need a couple of minutes to recharge after every use."

They crouched beside one of the few empty cells and took a moment to catch their breath. It was a very short moment. With the rhino men charging in their direction, Finn watched the gray-haired version of himself reach into his pants pocket and remove a small, flat disk no bigger than a silver dollar. He pressed a button on top and a stream of light particles swam over all four of their bodies.

"What's that?" Julep asked.

"A diversion." He peeked around a corner as the ranch hands approached, then tossed the disk down the aisle. It skittered along the floor and when it stopped, four lifelike holograms of them materialized. The illusions fooled the goons, leading them around a corner and away from the real group. A moment later, Old Man Finn darted over to retrieve the disk.

"Sick. If I had one of those, I would never go to school again," Lincoln said.

"Which is why Julep is going to be in charge of it," the old man said. He reached into the pajamas once more and took out a burlap sack. When he tossed the disk inside it, Finn heard a *clunk,* as if the bag held some secrets. The old man tied it with a string and pushed it into Julep's hands. "I'm sorry."

"Sorry for what?" Julep asked.

"Lots of things," the old man said, then looked at his watch again.

"We've got about twenty more seconds. Once the pajamas are recharged, shout the word *Playlist* and they'll take you to the first of the three dates."

"And you just want us to cause trouble?" Finn said. "That's how we help you save the universe?"

Old Man Finn nodded. "Get in, make Paradox angry, and get out as quickly as you can. There's nothing more to it."

"When it's over, we should go back to—"

"No. Don't!" the old man said before Lincoln could finish. "I know you, Lincoln. You want to see dinosaurs and cavemen and all that stuff, but the past is not a playground. If you mess something up, there's no telling what kind of damage you could do to the future."

"Isn't that exactly what you've been doing for the last sixty years?" Julep asked.

"Yeah, why is it okay for you and not us? There's things I'd like to change about the past," Finn said.

"Second-grade recess?" Old Man Finn responded.

"What happened in second-grade recess?" Lincoln asked.

"I wet my pants," the old man confessed. "I mean, we wet our pants."

Lincoln laughed.

"I couldn't hold it!" Finn cried.

"It's a memory I'm sure we would both rather not have," Old Finn said, "but leave it alone. Even adjusting one little thing can wreck the future. Just stick to the plan. But if something goes wrong and you get into trouble, you can override the pajamas' programming by calling out a specific date. Only go to places in the future, and whatever you do, don't take the pajamas off until Paradox is destroyed."

"Really? How am I supposed to go to the bathroom?" Finn asked.

"You'll figure it out. Listen, Finn, I'm serious. Don't take them off. While you have them on, the world is safe from the changes you make, but once you remove them, everything you've altered becomes permanent. Plus, you cause this nasty side effect," the old man said, gesturing outside at the storm.

A boom shook the Barn. Through an open window, Finn saw a wagon rise into the air and blow away.

Heavy footfalls approached. They seemed to be getting louder and louder and coming from different directions.

"They're trying to trap us. We need to keep moving," the old man whispered. He carefully crept around the corner and led them down the aisle. He was very quick for a seventy-year-old man. They zigzagged through the cells until they found a second ladder. Finn peeked over the ledge and his heart stopped. How had they climbed so high? He couldn't even see the ground. Heights unnerved him, and the creaking of the Barn against the storm made everything worse. He backed away from the edge even as more ranch hands approached.

"All right, it's either up or down," the old man said. "But we can't stay here."

"Up!" Lincoln swung himself onto the ladder.

Julep gave Finn's hand a squeeze as if she could sense his anxiety. "You can do this." A second later, she was climbing, too.

"Do I ever get over my fear of heights?" he asked his older self.

"Not so much," Old Man Finn admitted. "Just take some deep breaths and don't look down."

Finn moved hand over hand up the ladder with his face pointed forward. Suddenly, he realized the old man wasn't following.

"Come on," he said.

"No, kid. I've done all I can. Now it's your turn. It's up to you. When Paradox is dead, I promise to tell you where our dad is hiding. Come back here. I'll be waiting. Oh, one more thing. Don't go to the dome. You'll find nothing good there."

"Why? What dome?" Finn asked, but his voice was drowned out by the wind.

Angry ranch hands rushed forward and surrounded the old man, overpowering him with their numbers and strength. Others climbed the ladder after Finn and his friends.

"Hurry!" Julep shouted from above.

One of the rhino men grabbed his leg and yanked, nearly sending him flying off the ladder. It pulled harder. Finn heard a tearing sound and then lost his grip.

Before he fell, a hand wrapped around his wrist. When he looked up, he saw Julep holding him tight. Lincoln was holding on to her.

"Finn! You're too heavy. Climb back up," Julep begged. Her face was red. She couldn't hold him much longer, but his feet couldn't find the ladder. They kicked out into open air with nothing to support them.

"I'm losing you!" Lincoln shouted.

And then, all three of them fell like rocks toward the barn floor.

"Turn on the pj's!" Lincoln shouted.

"Right! Playlist!" Finn cried over the wind blasting his ears.

He felt energy building all around him. It caused his hair to stand on end, and then a golden sphere enclosed the trio. Just before they crashed to the floor, a hole appeared beneath them, and the bubble sank into it.

5

Zeke slid his metal bands back into the clamps that held them on his head. Old Man Finn stood nearby with his hands tied behind his back.

"Congratulations, Zeke. You finally caught me," the old man said. "I suspect there aren't too many people who have been able to hide from you as long as I have."

"Interesting how easy it was," Zeke said. "It was almost like you wanted to get caught. So what's all this about Foley?"

The old man grinned.

"You show up on the Ranch, bring a time twister down on our heads, help the younger version of yourself escape, and seeing as you aren't wearing the pajamas, I have to assume you gave the time machine to him."

The old man gave him a "Who, me?" expression.

Zeke shook his head. He couldn't help but admire the old man a little. Sure, he had been embarrassed by him time and time again, but Old Man Finn was clever. Zeke knew he would miss chasing him.

"Foley, I—"

"Call me Finn. We're old friends, aren't we?"

"Old friends don't kick each other in the gut," Zeke said.

"Sorry about that, but I couldn't let you get in the way. The kid is too important. And let's be honest, since when does a kick from a senior citizen like me stop you? You're a tough man, Time Ranger. If I didn't know any better, I might think you let the kids get away."

Zeke gave the ranch hands hovering nearby a glance and they left him and Old Finn to speak alone.

"The others might call me a fool and a softhearted idiot too eager to see the good in others, but it worked well for the man who wore this star before me."

"I suspect the others will call you a traitor now," Old Finn said.

"Maybe," he admitted.

"The mess I made was to stop that thing, Zeke. You know that."

"So now you've sent the boy and his friends with your mop?"

Old Finn looked down at his feet. Zeke knew the

conversation was painful for him. The losses were still fresh even after all these years. Changing the subject seemed like a kindness.

"I'll have to go after them," Zeke continued. "Consider yourself lucky that it's me and not one of the others. Perhaps you can repay the favor and tell me where you're hiding your father?"

The old man grinned.

"That would be a spoiler. Don't you want to be surprised?"

"I've never cared for surprises, Foley," Zeke said.

"I'll tell you my secret, but you need to do me a favor. If the boy comes back alive, point him in the right direction. I made him a promise. You're the closest thing I have to a friend in this universe. Will you help me keep it?"

Zeke nodded. "I will, but what happens if I catch him first?"

Old Man Finn chuckled. "We both know that's not going to happen, Zeke."

Below them, Zeke heard voices. The Rangers were charging into the Barn, and they were angry.

"If you have something to tell me, you better spit it out," he said.

The old man leaned in close and whispered the answer into Zeke's ear. The truth was so obvious he wondered why he hadn't considered it himself—or was he giving himself too much credit?

"Clever," he admitted. He couldn't help but laugh.

"High praise from a Time Ranger," Old Finn said. "You better put me in a cell now."

Zeke gestured for the ranch hands. They came forward, a few nursing bruises their prisoner had given them, and led Old Man Finn away.

"One more thing, Foley. Did you tell the boy the truth about Paradox?" Zeke asked.

He shook his head.

"I didn't have the heart."

A second later, he was gone.

Miss Ellie, Buford, and a handful of the Rangers reached the top of the ladder and rushed toward Zeke.

"Zeke! Is it true? You captured the older Finn Foley?"

"I've got good and bad news. The good news is yes, Finn Foley is in custody. The bad news is the younger version and his friends have escaped and they took the pajamas with them."

Thunder clapped overhead.

"This is a catastrophe!" Buford growled.

"I'll find him," Zeke said.

"And why do you expect us to trust you? You just spent half an hour arguing that we should let the kids go," the blob said.

"Anyone here that's questioning my integrity better

get ready to taste my knuckles," Zeke roared. "I pledged an oath to protect Time. Anyone who doubts it should step up and face me."

Miss Ellie gave him a hard stare. Her revolvers glowed. Zeke wondered if she was going to take him up on his invite.

"All right, Zeke. You go get 'em," she said. "Meanwhile, have Cookie insert the copycats right away."

"I hear they're busted," Buford said.

"They're all we have. Once Zeke catches the kids, we'll make new ones."

"I appreciate your faith in me, ma'am. I won't let you down," Zeke said.

"No, you won't let me down, Zeke. I'm going to make sure of it. You're getting a partner. I've summoned the Tracker."

Zeke's hearts stopped and he felt dread creep up his throat.

"The Tracker?"

"Yes, Zeke, and if Finn and his friends put up a fight, he has been instructed to bury them six feet deep."

6

Kate Foley's heart was bouncing like a rabbit. She had just finished watching the latest episode of *Unicorn Magic,* and it was epic! Starpower unlocked the final clue to opening the Tomb of the Golden Mane. Nightwhisper told Moonbeam about his feelings for him. Waterfall won the Stallion Cup, beating out all the other elementals, including Heatray and Ground-swell! Kate couldn't wait to talk to the rest of the Corn-ies. Tessa, Destiny, and Sophia were probably going crazy waiting for her to log in to their weekly group chat. Each Friday afternoon, after they watched the show online, the four girls talked for hours, discussing every detail. With her laptop in hand, she typed in her password and eagerly watched the screen for her best friends' faces.

Unfortunately, they weren't waiting. Destiny didn't answer, which was strange. When Kate tried Sophia next, it rang and rang. Luckily, when she tried Tessa, she logged in and said hello.

"OMG! OMG! OMG! OMG! OMG!" she cried. "Am I right?"

Tessa gave her an unenthusiastic nod. She looked distracted and uncomfortable.

"Seriously, aren't you dying? Aagh. I'm dead! It was so, so, so, so good. Have you heard from Destiny and Sophia?"

"Um, I think they're busy," Tessa said.

"Busy? Okay, should we wait?" Kate said.

"Um . . . I don't think so. They didn't watch it," Tessa said.

"Huh?"

"I didn't actually watch it, either," Tessa admitted.

"Tessa! How could you forget?" Kate asked, crestfallen.

"I didn't forget. I just . . . Why are you having a heart attack about this?" Tessa said.

Somewhere off-screen, Kate heard giggling. She watched Tessa shoot an angry look toward a part of her room the camera couldn't see. Someone was there with her. But who?

"What's going on?" Kate asked.

Sophia and Destiny stepped forward and lazily

waved at her. Both looked embarrassed and fell into more nervous giggles.

"So how were the unicorns?" Sophia asked.

"Don't be mean," Tessa said, shushing her.

"Whatever. The movie starts in fifteen minutes. Let's go," Destiny said.

"See you later," Sophia said. She and Destiny disappeared down the hall, leaving Tessa alone with her guilty expression.

Kate watched her fidget. A little voice inside her said it was all over for the Cornies. She had seen the same thing happen to other kids at her school. One day, groups of friends suddenly dumped one of their own, leaving that lonely kid confused and depressed. She never thought it would happen to her.

"I'm sorry," Tessa mumbled. "We all outgrew it a while ago and we didn't know what to say. Kate, it's a baby show."

Kate couldn't bear to hear another word. She slammed the laptop shut and sat in uncomfortable silence, going over the last few days in hopes of finding the clues she had missed—the subtle hint, the sarcastic comment, the obvious snarky suggestion she might have somehow ignored. Nothing jumped out at her. If Tessa and the others thought she was a baby, they'd hidden it from her very well.

Were they right? Sadly, she suspected they were. Her bedroom was a shrine to unicorns: posters, dolls, stuffed animals, T-shirts, games. She even had a unicorn stapler. She was obsessed, but could you blame her? She knew something the other girls didn't know. Unicorns were real.

She had seen them up close, talked to them, even ridden on one's back. She visited their world and begged them to help her save Earth. They'd made her an honorary member of their band. She was a Sister of the Bloody Hoof (unicorns were a lot more violent than she expected). They promised to sing songs of her bravery for generations to come. Seriously! How was she supposed to outgrow unicorns?

It seemed she didn't have a choice. The unicorns were on the other side of the universe. She would probably never see any of them again. She was here, on Earth, risking life as a friendless loser. Though it made her sad, she knew what had to be done.

Downstairs in the kitchen, she found a box of trash bags. When she got back to her room, she stuffed every unicorn object she owned into them: the porcelain doll collection; the beanbag buddies; the hoodies and T-shirts; the glow-in-the-dark window art; the curtains; her bedspread, sheets, and pillowcases; her rug; her pen-and-pencil set; even the Halloween costume she'd worn when she was four years old. Nothing was spared, no matter how much she cherished it. When she was finished, she counted fifteen bags filled to the top.

Getting them down the stairs and out to the curb was no easy task. She was exhausted. She stood over the bags, hating herself for being disloyal and changing so that others would like her. It felt shallow and gross. She was ashamed of herself. What would her unicorn friends, Deathkick and Blood Reaper, think if they ever found out? Would they sing a new song about her called "Kate Sucks"?

When she went back to her room, it felt empty. All the color was drained away. The only things left were her bed, a half-empty bookshelf, and her dresser.

"So this is growing up," she whispered to herself. She told herself it was the right thing to do. It was time to let go of all the childish nonsense. She was practically nine years old, for crying out loud! But she kept looking out the window at all those trash bags. She wanted to run down to the curb and drag them all back to her room.

WHOOSH!

The sound came from the hallway. It reminded her a lot of something she had heard before—a wormhole! It was followed by a bright light, too. She dashed into the hall, half expecting to find an alien or a robot or even a unicorn, but instead she nearly ran face-first into her brother, Finn, and his friends, Lincoln and Julep.

"Hey! Was that a wormhole?" she asked as she eyed them suspiciously. Finn had told her the wormhole generator was destroyed in the fight with the Plague, but he was known for fudging the truth. He was a genius at playing dumb, and now he looked dumber than ever. His eyes were glassy and his mouth hung open. Lincoln and Julep looked just as dopey.

"Something's up. I can tell. What are you keeping from me?"

Finn looked to Lincoln, who looked to Julep, who looked back to Finn.

"Meow," Finn said. Lincoln and Julep did the same; then the trio pushed past her and went into his room. They closed the door in her face before she could follow.

"Seriously?" Kate shouted. She gave Finn's door a good kick, then marched downstairs and into the backyard. For the last few weeks, Mom had turned the hammock into her study space. She was back in college, studying to earn a degree in library science. A librarian's degree was one of the hardest to get. Mom was expected to know a little bit about everything, or at least where to find answers. Most days Kate found her covered in a mountain of textbooks and highlighters. She and her brother tried to help. They made flash cards to get her ready for tests, but when she was in the hammock, they were supposed to leave her alone, unless there was an emergency. Kate's world was crashing down around her. It seemed like an emergency to her.

"I'm not a baby," she declared.

"Honey, I'm studying."

"Kate is a baby name. From now on I want you to call me Kathryn."

"Whatever you say, Kathryn, but I've always liked the name Kate."

"I need some new clothes."

"New clothes?"

"No pink," Kate said. "And I need new curtains, sheets, a rug, and a new bedspread. I threw them all out."

Mom set down the book.

"Okay, you get three minutes. What's this all about?"

"Am I immature?" Kate asked.

"Your grandmother used to have a saying. *Don't ask a question when you don't want the answer.*"

"Tessa, Destiny, and Sophia don't want to be my friends anymore."

"I'm sorry to hear that, Kathryn."

"And now Finn and his friends are teasing me, too."

"Honey, if it was any other day, I would drop everything and make you cookies, but—"

"Mom!"

"Very grown-up cookies. But I have a test today and I need every free minute to study for it. Can you wait to grow up until I get back tonight?"

"You want me to press pause on my epic sadness?"

"I think that's a little dramatic," Mom said.

Kate threw up her hands.

"Fine! Go back to studying! If you need me, I'll be in my room dying of a broken heart!" Kate grumbled. She turned and stomped back toward the house.

"I know you're feeling better because you're still sassy," Mom called out to her. "I'm leaving for class in five minutes. Tell your brother he has to stick around and look after you, but not babysit you, 'cause you're practically an adult."

Kate slammed the door behind her and marched up the stairs. When she got to her room, she gave the door an extra-loud slam so everyone would know she was unhappy. After several minutes, no one came to check on her, so she decided to slam the door again. When that didn't get a response, she stormed across the hall to Finn's room and threw open his door.

"Mom has her dumb test, so you have to stay here, but you're not babysitting . . ."

Kate's words faded when she saw her brother and his friends. Finn was standing on his bed, swatting at something that wasn't there. Lincoln was on his hands and knees, pawing at the curtains. Julep ran across the room and slammed into the wall face-first and knocked herself down. When they noticed Kate, they stopped and stared at her, let out another *meow,* then went right back to being weird. Why were they acting like cats? What was the joke? If they were going to tease her, the very least they could do was make sense. Stupid-heads! Dummies! She prepared to unload a string of insults, when she spotted a long white tail spill out the back of her brother's pants. It unrolled all the way to the floor, then flipped around like it had a mind of its own.

"Aaagh!"

She raced back to her room and slammed her door again. This time she locked it tight, then started pushing her furniture against it. She was shoving her dresser when she heard her mom's car outside. *Mom! No! Stop!* Kate rushed to the window, shouting and waving, but her mother didn't hear. She backed the car out of the driveway and disappeared down the road, leaving Kate all alone with . . . well, she wasn't exactly sure.

7

From inside the golden sphere, Finn, Lincoln, and Julep watched the strange environment flying by them. The bubble was rocketing through a translucent tube at an unbelievable speed, like they were blood cells racing through a vein. At times, the tube splintered off, causing the bubble to make sudden and jarring turns. There was no way of knowing where they were going, but there seemed to be thousands and thousands of possibilities. The bizarre network of paths existed within a swirling neon cloud of blues and blacks. Lightning flashed through its inky atmosphere, causing the colors to churn violently like hurricanes.

"It's beautiful," Julep said as she used her phone to take pictures of everything she saw. "I've read so many books on time travel. They all have it wrong. Who would have thought there would be alien cowboys, pj's, and a big golden balloon? I bet Albert Einstein would be so jealous of us. Finn Foley, you take me to the coolest places."

"Only you would find this fun," Lincoln said. "Where is this thing taking us?"

"You mean *when* is it taking us," Julep said.

"This isn't a game, Julep. Didn't that old dude say this thing was going to drop us in the middle of a battle with a monster? What are we going to do, throw your book bag at it?"

Julep shied away. She was very protective of her books.

"And why is it that every futuristic technology we get makes me barfy?" Lincoln continued. "Can you slow this thing down, derp? I'm about to upchuck all over our shoes."

"I'm not in control," Finn admitted. There were no buttons or levers inside the bubble. "Does anyone see a steering wheel?"

"No, but I see a clock," Julep said, pointing above them. A digital clock with a date and time was implanted in the sphere's golden skin. At that moment it read *8:18 a.m. February 14, 1835.*

"Whoa . . . 1835? Why are we going back in time?" Lincoln said. "Old Man Finn told us to stay away from the past!"

Finn eyed the clock. The date continued to roll backward. It didn't make any sense to him, either.

"Maybe that's where the first battle took place," Julep said to Lincoln. "Get that crazy laser weapon ready. What did he call it, again?"

"A Chrono-Disrupter," Lincoln said.

Finn studied the weapon. It was the strangest thing he had ever seen, shaped like a closed umbrella with a cantaloupe stuck on the end. On the bottom were a computer screen and a single blue button. It looked more like a prop from a cheap science-fiction movie than something they could use to fight a monster.

"What do you think it does?" he asked.

"*Chrono* comes from the Greek word *Kronos,* meaning 'time,'" Julep said.

"How do you know that?" Lincoln asked.

"A library card is a magical thing," she said. "We all know what *disrupter* means, so I guess your big blaster somehow disrupts time."

"You can call it whatever you want as long as it makes loud noises and blows stuff up," Lincoln said.

Suddenly, the bubble dropped its speed dramatically. The kids almost fell down.

"We're stopping," Finn said. The time and date were now rolling back at a snail's pace, until it was ticking off seconds. When the clock read *October 6, 1777,* the bubble was shot out of the tubes and everything went from blue to bright. Blinded, the kids tumbled over one another, slamming into the sides of the sphere and flopping around like fish in a bucket. When they regained their balance, they picked themselves up and looked out on the world. A field of wild grasses spread out before them in every direction. The familiar Hudson River snaked along to the east. Evergreen trees blanketed the mountains. A flock of wild turkeys sprinted away, startled by the bubble's sudden arrival. To Finn, it looked like home, but if the clock was right, it was a very different time period. There was also something he was expecting to see that he didn't.

"Anyone see a battle?" Lincoln asked. "Or a monster?"

Finn peered through the golden skin. There wasn't a soul as far as he could see.

"I don't hear anything, either," Julep said. "I was expecting . . . you know . . . noise."

"Maybe Old Man Finn challenged Paradox to a picnic," Lincoln said.

Julep turned to Finn. "Do you think there's a chance we're in the wrong time? Maybe he programmed the dates wrong by mistake."

"I honestly don't know. He didn't tell me much," Finn said. Maybe Julep was on to something. What if this was a mistake? It irked him. All he wanted was his dad. The old man was basically blackmailing him to help fight his stupid war, and worse, Finn had to do it while wearing the most embarrassing outfit ever.

POP! POP!

"What was that?" Julep asked.

"Sounded like someone is setting off fireworks," Finn said.

A second *POP!* rang out, then a whiz that passed by the bubble. It was followed by a third, but this time something smacked into the side of the sphere. Whatever it was ricocheted into the dirt. When Finn looked down at it, he saw a small black metallic object.

"Get down!" Lincoln cried, dragging his friends to their knees. "That's a bullet from a musket. Someone is shooting at us."

"And you know that how?" Julep said.

"I don't need a library card to see those men heading this way with rifles," Lincoln said, pointing toward the far end of the field. Finn strained his eyes. An army of soldiers charged toward them on both foot and horseback. They were dressed in long red coats and tricorner hats. They carried muskets and swords and roared a ferocious battle cry.

Another gunshot rang out, but this one came from behind the kids. When they turned, they found a second army approaching from the opposite direction. These soldiers weren't dressed as well as the first. Many were ragged and filthy. Some wore blue coats, but most were in long brown ones. A few carried muskets, but most held pitchforks and axes, as if there weren't enough weapons to go around.

"We're in the middle of the Revolutionary War," Lincoln said. "The guys in red are the British. The dirty guys are Americans."

"How do you know that?" Finn asked.

"The Hudson Valley was the scene of a lot of important battles. Why are you two questioning my intelligence? I know stuff!" Lincoln said. "I've been kicked out of some of the best schools in the county, thank you very much."

"It seems like the bubble is bulletproof," Julep said.

"Well, it might be bulletproof, but is it cannonball-proof?" Lincoln asked, pointing to the top of the ridge.

There Finn saw three soldiers wheeling a cannon into position. They stuffed one end with heavy balls, then poured black gunpowder into the back. When it was ready, they lit the wick and aimed the barrel right at the kids.

"I don't think I want to wait to find out. We need to move!" Finn cried.

Lincoln rushed to the sphere's wall and pushed against it with his shoulders in hopes of making it roll. Finn felt it teeter a little, but Lincoln wasn't strong enough to get the job done by himself. Julep seemed to read Finn's mind, and together they helped. It started out fine, but the faster it got, the clumsier the trio felt. Staying on their feet got harder and harder. Luckily, when the boom of the cannon mashed their ears, they were safely out of the way.

"They missed us!" Julep cheered as a shower of soil came down on the sphere.

"Save the celebration. Look!" Lincoln said, pointing to the other side of the battlefield. The Americans were rolling up their own cannon.

"Push the other way!" Finn said, and they rushed to the other side of the bubble. Once again, they narrowly missed an impact. Unfortunately, they pushed too hard and rolled themselves back toward the approaching British army. The ball pushed through the troops and stopped in the center of a mob of angry men. The British soldiers aimed their rifles at the kids, and the Americans joined them. Suddenly, the two armies were no longer interested in fighting one another. All of their attention was on the three children inside the golden ball.

"Come out of there," one of the soldiers demanded as he smashed the butt of his musket against the sphere's hard surface.

"Who are you?" another asked. "Spanish? French? Are you Dutch spies?"

"We're middle schoolers," Julep shouted, then turned

to her friends. "I don't want to freak anyone out, but Old Man Finn's bubble popped the second he showed up in the Barn, and ours hasn't. I'm not complaining, but . . ."

"It could happen at any time," Finn grumbled.

"C'mon, Julep! Why would that freak us out?" Lincoln cried.

"Sorry! Maybe it won't happen, but—"

POP! Julep's fears came true. The protective sphere vanished and the guns of two opposing armies were shoved in their faces. The kids slowly raised their hands over their heads.

"Kill them now! They're British spies!" an American soldier shouted.

"The Crown would never employ a filthy spy!" a red-coat called out. "They must be working for the colonies!"

"They're called states!" someone shouted.

The argument escalated, and the men turned on one another. Instinctively, Finn pulled Julep to the ground to avoid the fighting and pushing. He looked for Lincoln but didn't see him anywhere, until a honking sound filled the air. It startled everyone, but not as much as the sudden disappearance of the entire British army did. In the confusion, a single voice rose above the others.

"Sick!"

Finn spotted Lincoln not far from where he and Julep were huddling. The boy raised his Chrono-Disrupter and pushed the button. There was another honk, and in a flash the American army vanished, too, leaving Finn, Julep, and Lincoln alone in the field, aside from a few brave turkeys.

"Lincoln Sidana levels up!" Lincoln crowed while he pumped the weapon over his head. "Oy! Oy! Oy!"

"Lincoln! What did you do?" Julep asked after she got to her feet. "Where are the soldiers?"

"Did you kill them?" Finn cried in a panic. His heart was racing.

"No! Look!" Lincoln pointed to the flashing screen on the side of the weapon.

```
INVENTORY:
    2,003 British Soldiers
    2,018 American Soldiers
    1777 (American War of Independence)
    Cold Spring, NY, USA, Earth
```

"Wait? Are you saying they're inside that thing?" Finn asked as he pointed to the disrupter.

"There's one way to find out," Lincoln said. He turned the weapon toward a huge oak tree and pressed the button, and another honk blasted Finn's ears. A wave of energy erupted from the strange machine and a second later, the tree, leaves, and roots were gone, leaving a huge crater in the ground where it once stood. When the children checked the screen, an oak tree was added to the inventory along with the soldiers.

"Dude, you have to let them out," Finn said.

"I'm happy to. Just hand me the instruction book and I'll figure out how," Lincoln said.

"We can't kidnap four thousand soldiers. What if this battle was important to the war or something? We could mess up the future."

Lincoln shrugged. "Bummer."

"This isn't funny," Finn said. "Old me told us not to mess with the past and it's literally the first thing you did!"

"You know, I didn't want to come. I was perfectly happy lying in your backyard. You're the one that jumped up and followed a complete stranger into a magic portal. Instead of lecturing me, maybe you should thank me. I just saved our butts."

"That wasn't your plan," Finn said. "You just pushed a button. You had no idea what that thing would do."

"Stop bickering. You're like a couple of wet cats," Julep said. Her Southern accent got louder and thicker when she was angry. "There's no need to panic about the future. Old Man Finn told us that nothing we change in the past is permanent until Finn takes off the pajamas, right? So here's the easy fix: we move on to the next date. Hopefully, the old dude will be there fighting Paradox. We'll help and then he can tell us how to release the soldiers. Afterward we'll make a quick trip back here and put them where they belong. It shouldn't cause any problems for the future."

"If we find him. He sent us hundreds of years into the past. What if all the dates are wrong?" Lincoln asked.

"Why are you looking at me? This isn't my fault," Finn said.

"It is your fault. He's you!" Lincoln said.

"Stop bickering!" Julep cried. "We won't know until we move on to the next date."

"There's only one way to find out."

Finn scanned the empty field once more. He worried Lincoln was right. There was no sign of a monster, a fight, or an elderly version of himself. Did the old man mess up? What if the old man wasn't being honest with him?

"Are you ready? I'd like to get out of here as fast as we can," Finn said, pushing his doubts aside. He was doing this to find his dad. Maybe Old Man Finn couldn't be trusted. He had to find out for himself. When his friends gathered around him, he took a deep breath. "Okay, here we go. Playlist!"

Finn's hair stood on end and a new sphere formed around them. A moment later, 1777 was gone.

8

Zeke went outside to survey the damage. The storm devastated what was left of the Ranch. The roof on the Barn was completely sheared away. The outhouse, one of the tractors, and a half dozen hogs were missing. Miles of fence were nothing more than splinters. It would have to be completely replaced. Old Man Finn knew what would happen when he came to the Ranch. The storm was meant to keep the Rangers busy, just as he suspected.

"You Zeke?" a gruff voice asked.

He turned to find a man nearly twice his size standing behind him. He was bulging with muscles and dressed entirely in black, except for the bone-white bandanna, making his head look like a skull. Revolvers with pearl handles hung from his hips, and the biggest knife Zeke had ever seen was tucked into the man's belt. Next to him was a snarling beast that looked like the hyenas Zeke had once seen on Earth. Its red fur stood up on its arched back, just like those scavengers, but this one was four times as big. The beast's face wore a wild and ravenous expression, and ropes of drool hung from the corners of its mouth. It snapped and bared long yellow fangs as if the mere sight of Zeke were a hateful thing.

"I guess you're the Tracker," Zeke said. He had heard the stories. Folks said the Tracker wasn't born, that he escaped from a bad dream. Zeke extended his hand out of respect but was snubbed.

"Let's go," the Tracker said.

"You mean after Finn and his friends? We don't know where they went," Zeke said.

"The mongrel has their scent," the Tracker said. "We'll find them soon enough."

Zeke eyed the creature again. So this was a Time Hound. He had heard the stories but had imagined something a bit saner.

"Good. I reckon a conversation is in order before we head out," Zeke said. "I know Miss Ellie gave you in-structions on what to do with the kids when we find them, but—"

"I know my job."

"Listen, Tracker, I'm leading this hunt," Zeke said as confidently as he could. "I intend to capture Finn Foley without any bloodshed."

"What you intend and what is going to happen are entirely different things," the Tracker snarled. "You'd be wise to not interfere unless you want to meet the same fate. You got a problem with that, Ranger?"

Zeke locked eyes with the man, if the creature was in fact a man. Everything about the Tracker felt wrong. Darkness seemed to emanate from him. He was scarier than any Time criminal Zeke had ever hunted, and it was obvious that trying to reason with him was going to be a waste of oxygen. Zeke considered a confrontation, but it would get back to Miss Ellie. She'd force Zeke to stay on the Ranch and send the Tracker alone. He couldn't let that happen. Finn Foley had to live, and he had to make sure of it.

"No problem," Zeke lied. He removed his lasso from his hip and spread it out on the dusty ground. With a flick of the wrist, he whipped it round and round until it formed a perfect, spinning circle. The faster it went, the hotter it got, until the rope was on fire.

"Where are we going?" he asked.

The Tracker took off his glove and set his rough hand on the dog's head. Time Hounds could send messages through their thoughts, if you could get close enough to touch one.

"The year 1777. Don't have an exact day. Don't need one. The dog will pick up a stronger scent when we get there. Once the smell is planted in her nose, there's no place the guilty can hide."

"Okay, 1777," Zeke said, and a portal inside the rope circle appeared. The Tracker stepped through without hesitation, his Hound snapping at his boots. For a moment, Zeke was tempted to close the doorway and strand the man in the past, but no. For now, it was best to keep an eye on his partner. When the time was right, he'd find a way to stop the Tracker for good.

9

"**H**ere we go again!" Julep said.

Like their last time in the tubes, the clock spun backward instead of into the future. Years vanished in a flash.

"Old you is a moron!" Lincoln shouted at Finn. "Now where are we going?"

Lincoln was still in total jerk mode, but Finn understood his frustration. This didn't make sense. Was there a point to these trips, or were the dates mistakes? If Old Man Finn wasn't losing it, maybe he couldn't be trusted. The Rangers accused him of stealing technologies from the future. Maybe he was a liar, too. Maybe this whole programmed destination business was a way to keep Finn and his friends distracted. But why? He couldn't know, and it made him feel angry. He shouldn't have to be dragged through time, unsure of where he was going, just to find his dad.

Wait! Something was wrong with the pajamas. He bent down to get a better look at his pants leg and saw it was torn. A tiny black stain ringed the damage, and blue sparks shot out along the hole. It must have happened back in the Barn when the ranch hand snatched him. Oh, no! This was bad!

"We're going back to the prehistoric era," Julep said.

The bubble screeched to a halt, sending everyone head over feet. When Finn righted himself, he saw the digital clock read *8:17 a.m., August 8, 21,000,002 BC.* He glanced through the golden sphere. They were no longer in the tubes, but they weren't anyplace he recognized, either. Instead of the rolling hills of Cold Spring, he saw a wetland with pools of water and snow in every direction. He also noticed the sphere was about twenty feet off the ground.

POP! The bubble disappeared and the trio fell into the water. No one was hurt, but the landing won Finn a face full of muck. When he swam to the surface, he spit some out in disgust, but there was nothing he could do about the filth covering his body. Every inch of him was slick and slimy. Mud and weeds plastered his hair to his head, and the pajamas were soaked.

"Aaargh! Foley! I blame you for this!" Lincoln said as he conked some water out of his ears. He was just as messy as Finn. Julep had got the worst of it. Her glasses were covered with mud and she flailed around blindly.

They traipsed through the chilly puddles until they found a dry patch to stand on. Once there, the trio did their best to clean themselves up. When they were done, Finn studied their surroundings. The air was bitingly cold. Murky puddles stretched as far as he could see. Trees grew out of the water, and huge plants and bushes formed dense thickets. If he didn't know better, he might have thought they were on a different planet. And just like their previous trip to 1777, there wasn't a sign of Old Man Finn or Paradox anywhere.

"I don't know why we're here," Finn said before Lincoln could complain.

"Great!" Lincoln scoffed.

"Hey, this isn't his fault," Julep said.

"Then whose fault is it? He's wearing the time machine!" Lincoln turned his head and muttered something under his breath.

"Actually, it's these stupid pajamas' fault!" Finn said as he lifted his leg for his friends to see. "They're torn. I think it might be why we're not going where we're supposed to go."

"The pajamas are broken?" Lincoln said.

"Hey! Do you see me dancing for joy over here? I

didn't want to chase an old man through time! At least you don't have to wear this stupid outfit!"

"Yes, make it all about you," Lincoln shouted. "Just like always."

"Both of you need to shut your pie holes!" Julep whispered. "Anything could be lurking around here. We're going to attract attention if you two keep whining. The last thing we need is a bunch of cave people clubbing us on the heads and cooking us."

"I hope they eat him first," Lincoln muttered.

"Zip it!" Julep told him.

Finn could tell Lincoln had plenty more complaints, but Julep was scary when she was mad. Even the former bully didn't want to face her wrath.

Together, they agreed to search the area, just in case Old Man Finn was nearby. They traipsed through the mud and brush, feeling more waterlogged with every step.

"Are we sure this is Cold Spring?" Finn asked.

"I don't know. All the plants are wrong," Julep said. She pointed to a flower with a massive purple blossom. It was as big as a car tire. "Have you ever seen anything like that?"

"Doesn't smell right, either," Lincoln said, taking a big sniff. "Hey! Who beefed?"

"The one who smelt it dealt it," Finn said. Lincoln

was just the kind of person to poot and put the blame on someone else.

"Don't look at me!" Julep said as she pinched her nose.

"Seriously! It's coming from over there," Lincoln said, and without warning, he splashed through the water and into the forest.

"Lincoln Sidana, you stop right now!" Julep demanded, but the boy ignored her. They were forced to follow, but it wasn't easy. Walking through glacier melt was exhausting. Every few steps, they stumbled on ice and snow. For a moment, they lost Lincoln entirely, but then they heard his laughter. They found him standing in a clearing next to the biggest pile of poo Finn had ever seen. It was as tall as Julep, and easily the stinkiest thing to ever invade his nose.

"It's huge!" Lincoln said. His voice had an air of respect, as if he were looking at the work of a great artist. "Can you imagine how big the butt is that made it?"

"Classy," Julep moaned. Her face was looking a little green. The pile of yuck was making Finn dizzy, too. He needed to take a step back and lean against a tree just to keep his balance. With his hand on the rough bark, he felt an odd vibration.

"Hey, did you feel that?"

"Feel what?"

"There it goes again," he said. The second vibration

was followed by another and another. There seemed to be a rhythm to them, and they were getting stronger. He could now feel it in his feet and his belly, as if something was running in their direction—something really, really big.

"Is that an earthquake?" Lincoln asked when the trees started shaking.

"Lincoln, what did you just say about the poop?" she whispered.

"I said can you imagine how big the butt is that . . . ," Lincoln trailed off.

"What?" Finn asked. Now Lincoln wore the same worried expression.

"RUN!" Julep shouted, and she sprinted into the woods.

Finn and Lincoln didn't hesitate. They tore off after her, and together the trio darted through the trees.

"Why are we running?" Finn cried.

"Whatever made that poop is coming back, and it's bringing its big butt!" Julep explained.

The rest of the forest could sense what was coming, too. Panicked birds fled their nests, screeching in fear as they took to the sky. Hundreds of furry rodents scurried around Finn's feet. Tiny woodland animals, many he had never seen before, burrowed into holes in the ground. A sea of beetles and cockroaches spread across his path.

POUND! POUND! POUND!

Finn didn't know what was behind them, but he knew they couldn't outrun it. Better to hide. He spotted a huge boulder and pulled his friends behind it. They crouched together, doing their best to calm themselves and catch their breath.

"I've seen a lot of time-travel movies, and there are really only two possibilities for what is out there," Lincoln said. "The first is a T. rex, and if that's true, I'm afraid one of us is getting eaten. That's always what happens. Derp, you're the slowest, so it was nice knowing you."

"You're not helping," Julep scolded.

"It's not a dinosaur," Finn said.

"How do you know?" Lincoln asked.

"My dad and I used to go into the city to the Museum of Natural History," he explained. "They have a whole wing of dinosaur skeletons. There weren't many in this part of the United States, at least nothing on land. The big ones were in the ocean."

"Okay, not a dinosaur. I'm afraid the other option isn't any better. We aren't in the past. We're way in the future, when apes rule the world. That noise is an army of gorillas on horseback. They're coming to put us in cages."

A nearby tree exploded, and an enormous brown beast plowed its way past the kids and their hiding place. It stood nearly twelve feet tall from the top of its head to the bottom of its massive feet and smelled worse than the poop. The brute stopped abruptly and turned its muscular neck, revealing two massive curved tusks. It locked eyes on Finn and let loose with a heavy, aggressive huff from its long trunk. It wasn't his proudest moment, but Finn screamed. Julep and Lincoln did the same, and the trio held one another as they prepared to be gored.

For some reason, though, the creature didn't attack. Instead, it used its trunk to pull a sapling out of the ground and stuff it into its mouth. Finn watched it chew lazily. He and his friends seemed like nothing more than a mildly amusing diversion while it ate.

"It's a super-elephant," Lincoln whispered.

"It's a mastodon," Finn replied, remembering the museum again. His dad loved anything about history. They spent hours looking at ancient and extinct animals.

"Thank goodness my backpack is waterproof," Julep said, peering into it to check on her collection of books. When she was satisfied everything was safe and dry, she took out her phone and snapped a few pictures of the mastodon, all while grinning like an idiot.

"I would really love a selfie with it," she said.

"I want one standing next to the poop," Lincoln said.

"Maybe we skip the pictures and get out of here," Finn whispered.

Julep frowned but agreed. Just as the trio slowly

stood, three more animals leaped from behind the trees. These weren't as big as the mastodon, but they were just as scary. Each was like an overgrown cat—fast, savage, and golden. They pounced on the bigger animal's back with blinding speed. Their huge claws tore at its skin, and their sharp tusks dug into the mastodon's thick, hairy limbs. It cried out in shock and pain, then tried to shake them off. The cats held on tight, biting at its flesh.

"Saber-toothed cats," Finn breathed. "This is not good."

Lincoln gasped. "They're going to kill it!"

"We have to get away from here. Once they're done with it, they'll come after us," Finn said.

Without warning, Lincoln aimed his Chrono-Disrupter and fired. The mastodon vanished and the saber-tooths fell to the ground. They recovered quickly, and when they were back on all fours, they sniffed the air and turned their violent faces toward the kids. All three cats roared, crouched, and slowly crawled in their direction.

"Lincoln, why did you make the mastodon go bye-bye?" Julep said between heavy breaths. "The mastodon was our friend."

"I was aiming at the saber-tooths," he whispered.

"Are you going to try again, or do you need an invitation?" Finn asked.

"Oh, yeah," Lincoln whispered. He fumbled with the

disrupter, clumsily trying to activate it with nervous fingers. All the while, the massive cats inched closer and closer, their back legs tense and ready to pounce.

"Dude," Finn said. "Any time now."

"I'm trying!"

"I got this," Julep said. She reached into the burlap sack Old Man Finn had given them and took out the hologram disk. She pressed the red button and tossed it on the ground. Just as in the Barn, three perfect copies of the kids appeared. They drew the attention of the beasts, who leaped at them with open jaws eager for a feast—only to fly right through the children and land on the other side.

"Lincoln! C'mon," Julep said. "They're only going to be confused for a few minutes."

It was far less than that. All three cats took deep breaths through their noses, then turned their attention toward the real kids. Clearly, a scent was all they needed. The beasts sprang in unison. Lincoln pressed the button and a wave of energy caught the animals midleap. All three vanished, and the screen added the saber-tooths and the mastodon to the inventory.

"It's getting kind of crowded in there," Finn said as he leaned down to retrieve the hologram disk.

Lincoln shot him an irritated look, then sat down on a patch of soil. He looked exhausted and rattled.

"Okay, it's obvious the pajamas are wonky," Julep

said. "I don't like the idea of going off Old Man Finn's playlist, but he did say if we got into an emergency, we could go to another time. I vote that we go somewhere safe, like home. At least nothing is going to eat us there."

Finn nodded.

"Absolutely! Let's get out of here," he said, and he moved close to his friends. "Pj's, take us back home to the present." He announced the exact date, but nothing happened.

"Oh no," Lincoln said. "They really are broken."

"Has it been two minutes?" Finn asked.

"We've been here at least fifteen," Julep said. "Try the playlist."

"Playlist. Playlist? Plaaay-liiiist." No matter how Finn said it, nothing happened.

"Let's try something else. Try my eighth birthday," Lincoln suggested.

"Why?"

"On my eighth birthday my dad threw a huge pool party for me. My friends and I pushed the clown into the water. He was mad. It was hilarious. I'd like to see it again. Plus, we can take showers while the clown is threatening to sue."

Reluctantly, Finn tried Lincoln's birthday, but just like the other dates, nothing happened.

"We're not going anywhere. The pj's have a hole in

them. My guess is being soaking wet isn't helping, either," Julep said. "Let's find some shelter and give them a chance to dry."

It seemed like a good plan and they didn't have a lot of other options. Together, they walked for miles, maneuvering around pools of water and parts of the land that were impassable as they searched for a cave or anything that would keep them safe. Since there were no paths or roads, they weren't sure where they were going, and nothing looked familiar. Prehistoric Cold Spring offered no clues.

"I don't get it," Lincoln said. "If this is Cold Spring, where is the river? Where's Bear Mountain?"

"The Ice Age isn't over," Finn said. "The glaciers haven't created them yet."

After a couple of hours, they stopped to rest, though *relaxing* was out of the question. Everything in the forest seemed to be alive, chirping and growling at them from every direction. Finn was worried something big and hungry might sneak up on them, so they scurried inside a bush filled with blackberries as big as Finn's fist. Someone told him once that berries weren't always safe—many were poisonous—but he was starving. He plucked one, sniffed it, and decided to take the risk.

The first bite was amazing. It was a little like a blackberry, only slightly bitter. Purple juice ran down his chin and stained the front of the pj's. Lincoln and Julep decided to wait a few minutes to see if he got sick, then ate greedily. Finn ate three more before his belly was stuffed.

They settled into the bush and watched the sun set. They were wet, filthy, exhausted, and stained with berry juice. It was going to be a difficult night, but at least they were safe from anything that might want to eat them. Any creature who tried would have a tough time getting at them and would make so much noise the trio would have plenty of warning. The bush, however, did not protect them from the wind and the frightening cold that came once the sun was gone. To stay warm, they huddled together and shared body heat.

To take his mind off his misery and his chattering teeth, Finn thought back on those trips to the city with his dad. Sometimes they would spend half the day in the Museum of Natural History, then walk across Central Park to the Metropolitan Museum of Art. Dad loved history. The Egyptian room with the reassembled tomb was one of his favorite places to visit. He could wander around the Greek Hall and its collection of ancient statues for hours. Finn never cared much for the exhibits, but watching Dad get excited about old, dusty things made him smile. Funny; his dad had once accused him of not paying attention.

"You can't know the future unless you know the past," he had lectured, but some of what they'd seen had clearly found its way into Finn's brain.

"This time-traveling thing is weird. I keep thinking my parents and Truman must be freaking out wondering where I am, but the pajamas can take us back to the very moment we left. No one even needs to know we were gone," Julep said.

"*If* we can get back," Finn said.

"We have to get back. I can't let that goofy clone ruin my life," Lincoln said.

The copycats! Finn had totally forgotten about them. Were Mom and Kate home with that weirdness? What would happen if they figured out the copycat was an imposter? Were clones dangerous?

Worse, what if his family didn't notice? What if they were happier with a dim-witted Finn?

10

For the last half hour, Kate had been spying on her brother. Finn and his friends watched videos of birds on the internet while screeching at the tops of their lungs. He chased his strange white tail. From time to time, Lincoln whipped his head back and forth as if he were tracking something invisible. Julep sat on the bed licking the back of her hand, then using it to smooth her hair. They were always strange, but this was next-level bizarre. It was taking all Kate's strength not to freak out.

There was obviously something wrong with them, but she didn't have a clue what to do about it. She called her mom several times and left a dozen messages, but so far she'd gotten no response. She was probably taking her test. If there was anyone in the world who would know what to do about Finn, it was Mom. Until she called back, Kate knew it was up to her to keep everything under control.

She went back to her room and pushed her bed and furniture against the door, hoping it would be enough to keep Finn and his friends out. She could have kicked herself for throwing out all the unicorn stuff. Those fifteen bags were heavy, probably a hundred pounds combined, and a lot of it was pointy. They would have made an excellent barricade and weapons, too, unless space cooties made her brother super-strong. Space cooties was the only explanation.

She knew bouncing around the universe wasn't healthy. Six months ago, Finn and his friends were hanging out with robots and aliens, and she was sure none of them had washed their hands. There was no telling what kind of icky germs they brought back home. Plus, Finn and Lincoln were boys, and boys were famously disgusting.

With her barricade in place, she decided to do some research. Logging on to her laptop, she caught the frozen image of Tessa's face. Oh, yeah. She'd almost forgotten how the Cornies had dumped her that afternoon. Well, there was no time to feel sad about it now. She had bigger problems than a bunch of mean girls who thought they were too good for her.

She opened a search engine, hoping there might be

information on the internet that would help her, and started typing.

Big brother has tail

What came up was ridiculous. There were a lot of scary movies with dumb plots. She scrolled through them to find pages of a comic book about a cat super-hero. None of it was helpful.

People who act like cats.

Pages and pages of pictures appeared. People loved dressing like cats, especially at science-fiction conventions and on Halloween. Unfortunately, they led her to another dead end.

She tried *weird kids, people who lick their hands, cat craziness,* and *cat scratch fever.*

All of them were a waste of time.

"The internet is dumb," she said to herself, though she admitted she was asking the internet dumb questions. No one on Earth had a big brother with a cat's tail, or who had fought an alien invasion or visited another planet. There was no information on space cooties because no one had ever caught them. Kate was one of the only people on Earth who knew how weird the galaxy could be.

She heard the doorbell ring and jumped up to look out the window. It couldn't be good news. If Mom was back, she wouldn't ring the doorbell. Maybe a neighbor had seen the crazy stuff her brother was doing through his window. Maybe they'd called the men in sunglasses.

She opened the window and stuck her head outside. "Who is it?"

Tessa stepped off the porch and into view. "Kate?"

"It's Kathryn now. Kate is a baby name. What do you want?"

"I came over to talk. Are those bags on the curb full of your unicorn stuff?"

"What do you care?"

"Wow! You really had a lot," Tessa said.

"Go away. I'm busy," Kate said as she shut her window.

She watched her ex-friend wave and jump up and down at her. Tessa couldn't expect her to give her another chance, could she? But Kate's curiosity got the best of her and she opened the window again.

"I didn't go to the movie with Sophia and Destiny so I could come over and say I'm sorry," Tessa said. She looked around, embarrassed someone might hear her.

"Wait there!" Kate said, and she went to work moving the barricade. When she was free, she rushed down the stairs and threw open the front door.

Tessa was waiting.

"I feel bad about—"

"First, I am not forgiving you," Kate said.

"Okay."

"I want you to see something so you can take it back to the other Cornies, and I hope it makes you all feel terrible for dumping me."

"I didn't dump—" Tessa started, but Kate waved her off. She took her by the hand and dragged her into the house and up the stairs. When they were outside Finn's door, she got on her knees.

"What are we doing?" Tessa asked, copying her.

"So you can look through the keyhole."

"Why?"

"Just do it."

"This is your brother's room, right?"

"Yes."

Tessa cringed.

"If he's in his underwear, I really don't want to see that."

"Just look!" Kate demanded.

Reluctantly, Tessa pressed her face to the keyhole.

"You think I'm a baby because I like unicorns. The reason I like them is because they are real. I met a bunch of them and they made me an honorary member of their team. They helped fight an alien invasion. And yeah, aliens are real, too, and spaceships, and robots, and big ugly bugs with laser guns. The universe is full of strange things, and I've seen them in person! So no, I'm not going to outgrow unicorns!"

"Okay, that's an interesting story. What am I supposed to be looking at?" Tessa said when she pulled away from the keyhole.

"My brother and his friends. They've got space cooties!" Kate said.

"There's no one in that room," Tessa said.

Kate pushed open the door. Tessa was right. Her brother, Lincoln, and Julep were nowhere to be seen.

"Where did they go?" Kate wondered. She glanced at an open window. A breeze was fluttering the curtains. When she rushed to it and stuck her head outside, she almost screamed. Finn and his friends were crawling on the roof.

A second later, she and Tessa were crashing through the kitchen door and into the backyard.

"Listen, I came over here to apologize," Tessa said. "What we did wasn't very nice, and you didn't deserve it. I hope we can still be friends, but if you're going to try to make me feel dumb or play a prank on me, I'm not interested."

"Look!" Kate pointed to the roof. Finn, Lincoln, and Julep were prowling along the downspout, creeping up on a bird's nest. Her brother's tail flicked left and right with every step, and Julep was meowing. She turned her attention back to her friend. Tessa's mouth was wide open in surprise.

"I suppose you feel pretty dumb right now," Kate said.

11

Julep shook Finn awake, and he opened his eyes to a bright sun. The frosty night air was gone, but he could still feel the chill in his bones. He was stiff and achy. Sleeping on the cold ground was rough. He missed his bed and dry clothes and warm showers and soap.

"How long have you been awake?" he asked. Lincoln was nearby having more berries for breakfast.

"Awhile. We decided to let you sleep," Julep said. "I can't imagine what it's like in those wet pajamas. It seemed better for you to be unconscious than suffer. Do you think they're dry enough to give them another try?"

"Maybe. Let's get out of this bush," Finn said.

The kids scurried through the vines and got to their feet. Once there, Finn stretched and rubbed the sleep from his eyes. Lincoln snatched another berry and put it in his pocket while Julep slipped a handful into her backpack. Finn picked one for himself and munched on it as he studied the tear in his pj's. The black scorch marks around the hole were bigger than the day before, and the sparks were crackling.

"All right, let's give it a try," Finn said once his breakfast was gone. "Playlist!"

Nothing happened. He tried the word a few more times. He even shouted it, but it didn't make a difference.

"It's not the water. It's the stupid tear," Finn said.

"We have to fix it," Julep said.

"Great idea," Lincoln said. "Let me just get this needle and thread out of my pocket."

Julep rolled her eyes.

"Maybe there's something in here," she said as she opened the sack Old Man Finn gave her. "With the saber-tooths and swamp water, I forgot we even had it."

She untied the string that held it together and emptied it onto the ground. Finn and Lincoln hovered over her as she picked through the objects—the familiar hologram disk, a pair of glasses, a toothbrush, and a phone.

"I thought the Rangers said he was stealing technologies from the future. This is just a bunch of useless junk," Lincoln grumbled.

Julep picked up the glasses and studied them closely. She took off her own and put on the second pair. They were identical.

"What's wrong, Julep?" Finn asked.

"These are my glasses. They have the same frames and the same prescription," she said, then picked up the phone. "And this is my phone."

"Are you sure?" Finn asked.

Julep reached into her pants pocket and took out her phone. She laid it on the ground next to the other one. They were exactly the same. They even had the same scratch on the back cover.

"Turn it on," Lincoln said.

Julep tried, but the battery was dead.

"Why would Old Man Finn have my glasses and my phone?" she asked.

"Maybe he was keeping them safe for his Julep?" Finn said.

"I'm blind without them," she said. "And I'd rather die than hand over my phone. I need these things. Do you think something bad happened to me?"

"Actually, I've been wondering the same thing," Lincoln said. "If there's an Old Man Finn, where are Old Lady Julep and Old Man Lincoln?"

Finn watched their faces. His friends looked worried. He wished he had an answer for them, some kind of good news to put their minds at ease, but he didn't have a clue.

Julep abruptly collected the items and shoved them back in the sack.

"We don't have time to think about it right now. We need to fix the time machine. There's no needle and thread, so we've got to come up with another solution."

"Julep—"

"I don't want to talk about it, Finn."

He wanted to remind her what they'd learned on the Ranch: None of the things that happened to Old Man Finn and his friends had to happen to them. Their destinies weren't intertwined anymore now that their timeline was splintered. They were separate people, and their futures could be anything they wanted them to be. No one had to die. No one had to spend the next sixty years fighting a monster. But he let it go. Julep would talk when she was ready.

"All right, let's think. What can we use to fix torn fabric?" he asked. "Lincoln, could you please stop stuffing your face? Get over here and help us figure this out."

Lincoln had migrated to the bush for more breakfast. Maybe the thought of his impending doom made him hungry. He grumbled and threw a berry on the ground, or at least, he tried—it was stuck to his fingertips. It took him a few more tries before it finally went sailing into a bush.

"Geez, these things are sticky," Lincoln said.

Julep's face lit up.

"Lincoln, you're a genius!" she cried.

"I was trying to be subtle about it, but I knew you'd notice eventually," he replied.

She rushed to his side, took him by the hand, and led him to Finn. Once there, she smeared his sticky finger over the flap in the pj's, then delicately pressed the pieces together.

"It's like glue," Julep said.

"I think it worked!" Finn said. He could feel the energy growing inside the pajamas again.

"Well, what are you waiting for? An invitation? Get us out of here," Lincoln said.

"Playlist!"

A fresh golden ball materialized around them, and not a minute too soon. Another pack of saber-tooths leaped out of the brush. If the sphere hadn't blocked them, Finn and his friends would surely have been ripped apart by their claws and fangs. The bubble's skin was too strong, and the beasts fell to the ground, roaring with frustration.

"See you later, Garfield," Lincoln said to one of them.

Just as they were whisked into the tubes, Finn was sure he caught a flash of light in the corner of his eye. It looked like a ring of fire spinning in the air. Maybe it was his imagination, but he couldn't be sure.

12

Three hungry saber-toothed tigers were waiting when Zeke and the Tracker stepped into the Ice Age. The Hound fought off two of them, while her owner held the third by the throat. With his free hand, he drew one of his revolvers and fired. It wasn't a normal weapon. A stream of crystals shot out of the muzzle, encasing the enormous cat in a prison of ice. Two more shots and the others were trapped as well. The Tracker holstered his pistol, then scanned the horizon as if his near-death experience was already a distant memory. He whistled at the mongrel, and she went running off into the bushes.

"We just missed them," the Tracker explained. "The dog will find their scent."

"How does that work?" Zeke asked. "Can you hear her thoughts or something?"

The Tracker didn't answer. It didn't matter. Zeke had secrets, too. The steel bands on his head had a lot of functions. One of them helped him see the unmistakable energy scars that time travel left behind. He could literally see the changes Finn and his friends had made to the timeline. They were tiny and inconsequential this time, not like their last visit. Dragging four thousand soldiers away from a historical battle would have some nasty side effects in the future. This time, they added a mastodon and three saber-toothed tigers to the soldiers and the oak tree.

The Tracker was getting closer to finding Finn, and these near misses were amping up Zeke's anxiety and forcing him to plan what he was sure would be an unavoidable and violent confrontation with his partner. He also had to deal with an even bigger problem. Saving Finn and his friends would be seen as the ultimate betrayal to the Time Rangers, an organization he had vowed to honor. Miss Ellie would never forgive him. She and the others would strip him of his badge and lasso, and then what? Was he supposed to head back to his home world of Madonia? He'd left it hundreds of years ago. Everyone he knew was gone and buried.

Maybe this was a mistake. Was he letting his loyalty to Asher Foley get in the way of practical decisions? How could he turn his back on his son?

The Tracker whistled for his mongrel and she came barreling out of the brush as nasty and mean as when she disappeared. She dropped something black at her master's feet. It looked like a half-eaten piece of pre-historic fruit. The Tracker picked it up, sniffed it, then tossed it into the bushes.

"Tell me what you know about them, Ranger," the Tracker said to Zeke.

"You mean the kids? They're young, and clever for humans. They managed to fight back an invasion of their world by the Plague, and they outsmarted me for sixty years . . . at least, the first versions did."

"I'd hardly call that clever," the Tracker replied. He and his Hound stared with contempt at Zeke, making him nervous that the dog's psychic abilities might also include mind reading. The beast bared her fangs and growled.

"Filthy, rotten—" The Tracker pulled his weapon, turned it on Zeke, and fired.

"Wait!"

He prepared to be encased in crystals, but the blast flew over his shoulder. When he regained his bear-ings and collected his hat, he realized he hadn't been the Tracker's target at all. Suspended in midair was a fourth saber-tooth. The weapon caught it just as it leaped off a ridge toward Zeke. If the Tracker hadn't stopped it, the cat would have eaten him for lunch.

"I just saved your life. If you expect me to make it a habit, go back to the Ranch."

His hard eyes sent a chill through Zeke; then he gestured to the dog.

"Have at it," the Tracker said. He fired his revolver again, freeing the frozen cat. It fell to the ground, dazed, and the horrible Hound leaped on it, biting and ripping at its belly.

"The fugitives have moved on to March 3, 2069, around three-thirty p.m.," the Tracker said over the noise.

Zeke knew that date well. It was the day of one of the biggest battles Finn and Paradox ever fought. He'd spent days cleaning up that mess. But why would Old Man Finn send the young one there? It couldn't be a coincidence, unless . . . No, nothing the old man did was by accident. He always had a plan, and Zeke was starting to understand.

"What are you smiling about?" the Tracker grunted.

"Forget it," Zeke said. "You wouldn't find it funny."

13

"**S**o next time remind me not to complain about the broken time machine," Lincoln said as an explosion mashed their ears. A building collapsed only a few yards from them, forcing the trio to run.

When Old Man Finn gave them the pajamas, he'd told them they would appear in the middle of a fight. He hadn't exaggerated. Fires burned out of control. Smoke stung their eyes. The sky was a polluted soup of angry clouds, sulfur, and fumes from burning tires, but it seemed Finn and his friends were finally at one of the programmed dates. Just before the protective sphere vanished, the digital clock blinked *3:30 p.m. March 3, 2069,* and the words *Battle Number One.*

"Are we in Cold Spring?" Julep said.

It was hard to tell. Everything looked wrong. The

asphalt on the street buckled like waves on a rocky sea. Houses were nothing more than piles of glass, twisted plumbing, and broken two-by-fours. On the corner, Finn saw a fire hydrant spraying water fifteen feet into the air. Downed electrical wires twisted in the road like angry snakes, setting fire to everything they touched.

"Yep. There's your house, derp," Lincoln said, pointing to one of the piles.

Finn eyed it closely. He couldn't be certain—there was too much wreckage. A massive pine tree on the front lawn had somehow managed to survive, but there hadn't been a pine tree in his yard when he'd lived there. He scanned the street for clues. Wait! Was that Ms. Pressman's house? No, the front yard was all wrong, and her house was blue, not yellow, but . . . yes! It was her house. The windows and front door were the same. There was no denying it any longer: this was his street in the future.

"Mom! Kate!" He dashed toward the mess he had once called home, shoving wood and plaster aside with his bare hands, panicked that his family might be trapped under the debris.

"Finn! Stop!" Julep shouted as she pulled him away. "It's 2069."

"They're long gone!" Lincoln said.

"It's 2069," Finn said, trying to force his brain to accept the date. Almost fifty years had come and gone since he last stood on the porch. There was no way his mom and sister still lived here. At least, he hoped.

Another explosion rattled his teeth. This one broke windows in the few houses still standing, even though its source was at the far end of the block. The trio wasn't close enough to see what caused it, but a thick cloud of black smoke drifted up to the tree line.

"I think we found the old man," Lincoln said.

"And the monster," Julep said.

"C'mon!"

They sprinted toward the chaos, hopping over trash cans and fallen trees in the street. When they got to the corner, all three froze. Paradox was standing in the middle of the road. Its arms were extended wide and lightning crackled from its fingertips. Despite its lack of facial features, its rage could still be felt.

Finn wasn't prepared to see it in person. It was so much more frightening than the movies in the Campfire. It was like something that crawled out of a scary book, only real, bitter, and swollen with power. Everything in him screamed "Get away."

Without warning, Lincoln tackled him and Julep, and the three fell behind a pickup truck.

"What is wrong with you?" Finn yelled.

"You can't just stand in the road staring at it like a couple of dummies!"

"I couldn't help it," Finn said.

"Listen, we need to stay as far away from that thing as we can. Old Man Finn didn't tell us to attack it. We're here to be a distraction." Julep peeked over the truck bed for a second, then ducked back down just as quickly. "Any ideas?"

"You're asking me?" Lincoln said.

"He sent us here to be troublemakers!" she said. "You're the expert. What would you do?"

This time Lincoln poked his head over the truck.

"Okay, the street slopes down toward that ugly thing, and it's a clear path all the way. I say we roll this truck at it."

"You want to hit Paradox with a truck?" Finn said.

"Yep," Lincoln said. He crawled around the side, reached up, and tried the handle. The truck door swung open, and he gestured to Julep. "Get in."

"What? Why?"

"Because someone has to steer the truck so it crashes into the bad guy," he said.

"Why do I have to do it? You steer the truck," Julep said.

"Because I have to push it," he snapped, then gestured to Finn. "And he has to help me."

"Are you saying you two are stronger than me? I carry a twenty-five-pound backpack full of hardcover books everywhere I go. I'm probably stronger than the two of you put together!"

"She's got a good point," Lincoln said as he turned to Finn. "You steer."

Finn frowned but did as he was asked. Once inside, he crouched in the seat so Paradox couldn't see him through the windshield.

"Do you see the gearshift? Pull it toward you and then down so the truck goes into neutral."

Finn did as he was told.

"Yes, just like that!" Lincoln shouted to him. "All right, here we go."

Julep and Lincoln pressed their hands against the bumper and pushed. The truck nudged forward.

"Put some muscle into it, Li," Lincoln complained.

"I am!" she cried.

They pushed harder. After a few more groans and grunts, the tires started to roll.

"We're doing it! Don't stop," Lincoln said.

"How did you learn to do this?" Julep asked.

"Let's just say it was part of the reason I got kicked out of the Poughkeepsie Day School."

The truck picked up speed so that pushing was no longer necessary. Finn sat in the driver's seat, his knuckles white from clenching the steering wheel. He turned it to line the front bumper up with the raging monster, then adjusted it so that the truck was perfectly aligned.

"Okay, what now?" Finn shouted, but he got no

answer. When he looked back through the window, he saw his friends racing after him, but they were half a block away. "Oh boy."

The truck bucked over the damaged pavement. Paradox didn't notice it at first. It was so caught up in its violent tantrum that by the time it did see the vehicle, it was too late. The front end plowed into its chest. The impact sent the creature sailing into the air. It crashed down hard on the pavement several yards away and lay very still.

Finn slammed on the brakes. A moment later, his friends caught up and helped him out of the truck. Together, they hurried behind a mailbox and watched Old Man Finn and another elderly man attack the fallen monster. Together, they fired weapons that buried it in what looked like fast-drying concrete. In a matter of moments, Paradox was encased in stone.

"Is that me?" Lincoln whispered as he pointed to the other man. "How did I get a mechanical leg?"

"Let's get out of here," Julep said.

"Yeah," Finn said, clearly shaken. "Playlist!"

The sphere enveloped the trio, and a moment later, the old men and the monster were gone.

"**Y**ou think they have space cooties?" Tessa asked.

Kate nodded. It was the only explanation, and now that she had revealed everything about the last six months to Tessa, she was sure her former friend would agree.

"But the government said it was just special effects for a movie," Tessa said. "They shot a scene where the robot fought the giant bug downtown."

"It wasn't a movie," Kate said. "It was real, and now my brother and his dumb friends are sick. I mean, they're usually pretty weird, but this is a lot."

"What should we do about it?" Tessa asked.

"We are not going to do anything about it. You're going home," Kate said.

"Home? Why did you tell me all that stuff just to send me home?" Tessa asked.

"Because I wanted you to know what it feels like to have a huge secret you can't tell anyone," she said. "And trust me, if you do tell, the men in the sunglasses will come to your house, and I don't know what they'll do, but it will be bad."

"But I want to help."

"We're not friends anymore. You don't need to help me," Kate said.

"Kate!"

"It's Kathryn."

"Stop it. I came over here and apologized in person. I told you I felt sorry about what happened," Tessa said.

"I would hate to take you away from Sophia and Destiny," Kate huffed.

"Now you are being a baby."

Kate grumbled. Tessa was saying all the right things, and she did look regretful. It would be very satisfying to make her suffer some more, but that was something a little kid would do. She was mature now. She needed to be the better person.

"Your betrayal is forgiven," Kate said.

"Thank you," Tessa said. "Now, what are we going to do?"

"I don't know! My mom handles all the grown-up problems around here."

"Your mom knows what to do about space cooties?"
Kate shrugged.

"I guess we should probably try to get them back inside. What if they're contagious? They could infect everyone. I can't have a tail in the fourth grade. It will ruin my life," Kate said.

The girls looked up at the roof. The weirdos were still there, but now the bird's nest was empty and they were all licking their hands.

"They ate the bird!" Kate moaned.

"They're acting kind of like Stevie." Tessa's cat, Stevie, was a hateful thing. He wouldn't let anyone pet him, and he had no interest in playing with anyone, either. Once, Kate put him on her lap and Stevie had gone to the bathroom on her leg. Most days, he lurked around the yard, hunting birds and mice and hissing at people walking down the street. Tessa was right. Finn, Lincoln, and Julep were acting like cats. It explained the meowing and swatting at curtains and running back and forth for no reason. It also explained Finn's tail.

"What do you do when Stevie gets up on the roof?" Kate asked.

"We'll do what my dad does. Get the hose."

15

The clock shot forward more than a hundred and fifty years, stopping at 12:15 p.m. February 18, 2220. Unlike the last readout, this one did not say it was the location of the second battle. Finn hoped it was, but he wasn't holding his breath. The sticky juice holding together the tear in the pajamas was coming apart.

When the future materialized around them, the bubble was smack-dab in the center of a ten-lane highway packed with speeding cars. The trio's sudden arrival produced a symphony of screeching tires and angry honking, but the children were too shocked to try to roll out of the way.

"Let me guess. The jammies are out of whack again, right?" Lincoln said.

"At least we finished one of the dates. We only have

two more to go," Julep said. Finn appreciated that she was trying to sound positive, but her face couldn't hide her irritation.

"Guys!" Finn said in a panic. A car was on a collision course with them, and it didn't look like it was going to miss. They braced for impact only to watch two rockets blast the vehicle into the air. It effortlessly sailed over them and landed safely on the other side. Still, the driver rolled down her window and made an angry gesture.

"The future is crowded," Julep said.

"And cranky," Finn said.

"C'mon, we're wasting time. Obviously, Paradox and Old Man Finn are not here, but this place isn't a total loss. If we can find a store, we can buy a needle and thread and fix the tear in the pj's," Julep said.

"Sounds good to me," Finn said. "And maybe get something to eat."

"Hello. Can we talk about our shopping spree once we push the bubble off the road? I barely avoided peeing my pants when the car jumped over us. If it happens again, I can't make any promises," Lincoln said. "Oh, great. Here comes a truck."

The word *truck* didn't really explain what was coming their way. The monstrous machine was as big as an eighteen-wheeler, and it blasted a thick cloud of black pollution behind it. Finn braced for it to jump over them. Luckily for Lincoln's pants, it didn't try. When it was a few feet away, it came to a screeching stop.

"That's weird," he said as he peered closer. No one was driving it. In fact, many of the cars whizzing past them didn't have anyone behind the wheel. Finn had heard self-driving cars would be the future. It seemed to be true.

A huge metal arm on top of the truck swung directly overhead and dipped a claw down to pluck them off the road. Finn felt like one of those cheap plushies in an arcade game.

"What's going on?" Lincoln asked.

"I don't know. Maybe it's clearing the highway of trash. And we're trash," Julep said.

The arm lifted them into the air and swung them over the back of the truck. It dropped them into a square opening cut into the top. The fall knocked them around a little, but they were otherwise fine. Unfortunately, the arm wasn't satisfied. Their bubble was too big for the truck's hole, so the claw tried to force them in with the rest of the trash. When that didn't work, it tried pulling them out. That failed, too. Now the kids and the sphere were lodged in the opening. The arm pushed and pulled, but eventually gave up and swung back into position. A moment later, the truck lurched forward, zigzagging through traffic until it veered onto an off-ramp.

Finn scanned the horizon, hoping for a clue to where they were going. He spotted a huge field covered in a haze of smoke. Enormous firepits were lined up in rows that seemed to go on for miles and miles. A truck exactly like the one they were inside was parked next to one of the pits. Its arm reached into its back and snatched a claw full of debris. It swung the mess over the pit and dumped it into the fire.

A nervous bead of sweat rolled down Finn's forehead. The sphere was musket-ball-proof, and sabertooth-proof, but what about fire? He had his doubts. Whenever they landed in a new time period, he immediately felt the temperature outside the bubble. In the Ice Age, he'd shivered the moment they arrived.

"I've got some bad news," he said.

"I am sick of your bad news!" Lincoln said.

"Look!" Finn said, pointing toward the fires.

"What's going on?" Julep asked.

"Oh, the usual. We're going to a barbecue and we're the hot dogs," Lincoln grumbled.

The truck found a spot in front of a burning pit, and its mechanical arm went to work dislodging the bubble.

"What if this thing pops?" Lincoln asked.

Julep swallowed hard.

"How much longer before we can use the pj's?"

"Thirty seconds. Maybe more," Finn said. He could only guess. The digital clock always stopped when they got to their destination. He had no idea how long they had been in traffic world.

The clamp adjusted its grip and pulled. It changed position and tried again. Finally, on the third attempt, it wrenched the sphere free and swung it directly over the flames. Finn could feel the heat on his feet, even with his shoes on. He suddenly understood what it felt like to be a marshmallow.

The claw released its grip and the bubble fell.

"Playlist!" Finn shouted.

"Finn!" Julep cried.

"PLAYLIST!"

As the flames singed the golden globe, the world went sideways, and they were back in the tubes. Finn watched the clock spin backward a hundred years, then two hundred, until finally, *bam!* They materialized in the middle of Finn's street. With eyes as wide as moons, he and his friends each tried to catch their breath, but a car horn sent them all into a panic again. Luckily, it was just a man in a van. He veered around them and onto the sidewalk to avoid a crash.

"Get out of the road, you idiots!" he shouted at them as he drove away.

Finn glanced around. Unlike their first visit to his neighborhood, they weren't in a battle zone this time. In fact, there was no hint of the destruction they'd witnessed. The street and the houses and the lawns were all in good shape. The only difference was a For Rent sign propped outside his house. It looked empty. The windows were dark. Something told him no one lived there.

The exhausted kids wandered over to the curb and sat down.

"We have to get the pj's fixed right away," Finn said as he pointed to his pajama leg. The black ring around the tear was twice as big. "Maybe we can find a needle and thread here. I'd take you inside my house, but we don't live here yet. We're still living in Garrison at this time. That's a serious walk."

"What year is this?" Julep asked.

"The clock said 2015," Finn said.

"Yeah, my family is still in North Carolina. We didn't move to Cold Spring until my brother got sick a few years ago. His doctor is one of the best in the world, so we moved here to be closer to him."

"What day?" Lincoln pressed.

"Huh?"

"What's the exact date?"

"I think it said May third," Finn replied.

Lincoln's face went pale. He jumped to his feet and without another word sprinted down the street.

"Where are you going?" Finn shouted.

"C'mon," Julep said, and together they ran after their friend. For a big kid, Lincoln was surprisingly fast. When Lincoln was a bully, Finn had never been able to outrun him. Luckily, Finn knew the neighborhood, and it wasn't long before he realized where his friend was headed. He and Julep found Lincoln standing in his front yard, peering through a huge picture window.

"He's so weird," Finn said.

"No, he's not." Julep seemed to know something Finn didn't. It made him oddly jealous. She turned to Lincoln. "You okay?"

"It's me," Lincoln said. Through the window, Finn saw Lincoln's dad, Dr. Sidana. On his lap was a chubby five-year-old boy. He bounced and giggled like he was a cowboy on a bucking bronco.

"Little Lincoln," Finn teased. "You were cute. What happened?"

If Lincoln heard, he didn't respond. His full attention was on a woman. She was short with a sweet face. She scooped up little Lincoln and gave him a loving hug. The little boy hugged her back.

Lincoln went from looking stunned to smiling, to fighting back tears, to smiling again.

"Mom," he whispered. "I forgot what she looked like. I mean, there are pictures of her all over the house, but in my mind I forgot."

Julep reached into her pocket and took out her phone. She handed it to Lincoln.

"Take some pictures."

"Lincoln, maybe we shouldn't be here," Finn said.

"Today is the day she died."

Finn bit his lip. He couldn't think of a single word to say, so he didn't. He stood silently, hoping Lincoln could sense him there, hoping somehow his presence was making things better.

The trio watched the family for a long time. Every once in a while, they ducked away from the window so no one would see them. At one point, little Lincoln was too fast and spotted them outside. He pressed his face against the glass and made faces before he ran off to play with a Slinky on the staircase.

"I'll be right back," Lincoln said as he walked to the front door.

"Lincoln?" Julep asked. "What are you doing?"

"Tonight my mom gets in her car," Lincoln said, gesturing to a white Jeep parked in the driveway. "She goes out to get me some pancake mix for breakfast. I loved pancakes. They were all I would eat. On the way back, a truck runs a red light and she never comes home."

"I can stop it from happening."

Finn and Julep stepped between him and the doorway.

"You can't," Finn said.

"I *can*," Lincoln said. "We have a time machine. What is it for if not this?"

"Old Man Finn told us not to mess around with the past," Julep reminded him. "We don't know the consequences."

"I do! I'll get my mom back. I'll be happy. My dad will be happy. I'm willing to risk it," he said.

"This isn't just about you," Julep pressed. "If your life changes, you might never come to our school. We might never meet you."

"No offense, but I'll trade the two of you for my mom," Lincoln said. "Don't look at me like that! What if you had the chance to change something? Julep, what if you could cure your brother? Finn, what if you could snap your fingers and get your dad back? Wouldn't you do it?"

"Dude, you don't get it," Finn said. "Lots of good things have happened because you were around. We would have been shot by those soldiers for sure. The saber-tooths would have eaten us. We probably wouldn't have stopped the Plague invasion!" Finn said.

"You're both smart. You would figure those things out without me," Lincoln said.

"But what if we didn't?" Julep asked.

"That's not fair, Julep!" Lincoln shouted.

The light on the porch came on and the door opened. Lincoln's mom peered out at them with a confused expression.

"Can I help you?" she asked.

Lincoln opened his mouth. Finn expected their whole weird story to pour out, along with a warning to stay home that night, but Lincoln couldn't seem to make his mouth work.

"I . . . I think we have the wrong house," he finally stammered.

"Oh," his mom said, then peered closer at him. "Are you okay? You look very upset."

"Allergies," he said with a laugh. "Sorry, have a good night."

His mom nodded, then closed the door. A moment later, the light went out and Lincoln stomped toward the street. Finn and Julep went after him.

"Lincoln, I know this sucks, but—"

"You don't know anything!" Lincoln shouted when he spun around. He snatched Finn by the front of the pajamas and looked like he was ready to punch him. "We're jumping around in time so we can find your dad. When this is all done, you get him back. Have you thought about how that might suck for me and Julep?"

"Lincoln, it's not that simple," Julep said.

"It actually is that simple! We can change history for Foley, but not for us."

"You're right, Lincoln," Finn said. He squirmed away from Lincoln and snatched the Chrono-Disrupter hanging from his belt. He didn't even think before he pushed the button. The energy wave slammed into the Jeep, and in a flash it was gone.

"Finn!" Julep gasped. "What did you do?"

When the porch light came back on, the kids sprinted into the shadows, racing down the street with their hearts pounding until they were far enough away to stop. On the corner they bent over to catch their breath.

"Why did you do that?" Julep said.

Finn looked at Lincoln. He was a pain most of the time, but he was the best friend Finn ever had.

"If she doesn't have a car, she can't go out for pancake mix," Finn said. "It's a thank-you for coming with me. You should get something out of this. You both should. It's my fault we're out here. I'll deal with the consequences later."

"For everyone's sake, I hope they're worth it," Julep said.

Finn turned to face Lincoln. The boy looked like there were a thousand words in his mouth, desperate to get out, but they were too jammed up to break free.

"I hope so, too," Finn said. "We need something to fix the pj's, but the police will be here before long, and honestly, trying to explain what we did with his mom's car is not going to be fun. Not to mention one of us is wearing a pair of cowboy pajamas. Let's move on to the next date. Maybe we'll find an answer there. All right. Playlist!"

As a fresh bubble encircled them, Finn closed his eyes.

I've given up so much. Don't take Lincoln, too, he thought. He wasn't sure who he was asking; maybe Time itself. *All right, Time. I'm begging you. Don't take my friend away from me.*

16

February 18, 2030. Just below the date and time were the words *Battle Number Two.* Finn didn't know how to feel about it. The date was one step closer to finding his dad, but after their first run-in with Paradox, he wasn't sure he had any courage left.

"Here we go," Julep whispered, as if she shared the same worries.

They materialized right where they left, a half block from Lincoln's house. Unfortunately, it sat at the top of a steep road, and February 18 was suffering through an epic snowstorm. Six inches of white powder were on the ground with more falling from the sky. The sphere lost its traction and rolled down the hill, slowly at first, but when it hit a patch of ice, it picked up speed.

"This is not good!" Lincoln cried.

The kids bounced around inside the bubble, shouting and moaning whenever they slammed against the walls, but bruises weren't their biggest worry. A busy intersection was just ahead. They blasted through a red light, nearly getting crushed by a delivery truck.

"I'm ready to say it! I am not a fan of this time machine!" Julep said.

They zipped past a Chinese restaurant, a place that sold fancy camping equipment, and a bed-and-breakfast. One antiques shop after another whizzed by, then the ice cream shop and then another ice cream shop.

"There they are," Lincoln said.

It was nearly impossible to focus, but Finn could see a fire truck lying on its side and a burned-out police car. The ball rolled past them, through a battle between Paradox and three adults. They were so busy with their destruction, they didn't notice the enormous golden ball skidding down the street.

"And there they go," Finn groaned.

The fight was suddenly not their top priority. The train station was at the bottom of the hill, and an approaching locomotive blasted a warning horn. The kids rolled over the tracks and the 4:14 to Grand Central Terminal clipped them, sending the bubble high into the air. It came down on the other side and picked up even more speed. When the trio stopped screaming, they realized they were headed straight toward the Hudson River.

"We have to stop this thing or we're going for a swim!" Finn warned.

"We'll freeze to death long before that," Julep said.

They skidded through a patch of ice, which stopped the spinning. Finally, the kids were able to stand, though they were dizzy and nauseous.

"Help me push!" Lincoln rushed to the side of the bubble and pressed his shoulder against it.

"Why?"

"We need to steer toward the gazebo!"

Finn glanced down the road. The end of the street formed a circle, with a beautiful wooden gazebo in the center. Finn's mom told him once that his dad proposed to her on its steps. Even in the future, the town's favorite landmark was still standing.

"But we'll crash into it," Julep said.

"Better than becoming a Popsicle," Lincoln said.

Finn and Julep saw his point, and together the three pushed as hard as they could, but it did them little good. Steering it toward the gazebo also steered them toward the curb, and when the bubble hit it, they went flying into the air again. Up, up, up they soared, taking off the gazebo's roof and coming down hard on the other side. It didn't slow them down at all.

Now there was nothing between them and icy water

except a snowman someone had built on the pier. It exploded in a flurry when they hit it, and then *POP!* The bubble was gone. The kids fell to the ground but kept sliding closer and closer to the river. Finn clawed at the ground with his bare hands, trying to slow himself, but nothing he did helped.

"Aaaaaghhh!" they cried in unison as they hit a patch of asphalt. It wasn't slick, and slowed them to a sudden and painful stop just as their feet slid over the end of the pier. They lay there for a moment, breathing hard and saying prayers as sheets of ice drifted past them on their way to the Atlantic Ocean.

"We're alive!" Lincoln shouted. He paused for a moment and looked to the others. "Right? We're alive?"

"For now," Finn said, gesturing over his shoulder. The sounds of the battle were as clear as day five blocks away.

"Let's do this. I'm freezing to death," Julep said. She was shaking like a leaf. It had been a warm, sunny day when their adventure started. None of them were dressed for a blizzard.

"C'mon," Finn said. The kids raced back the way they'd come, heading toward the fight. When they got there, several police cars were approaching. Fireballs formed in Paradox's hand, and it pitched them at the police. The deputies inside had only seconds to leap to safety before their cars exploded. One flew into the air and came back down on its roof. In the havoc, three figures led an attack on the monster. One of them held what looked like a flamethrower. It sprayed Paradox. Finn squinted at the heroes and realized they were versions of themselves as young adults.

"We are pretty awesome in the future," Lincoln said. "Is that me with the flamethrower? Julep, take a picture."

His friends might have thought what they were seeing was fascinating, but Finn was horrified. Again, the old version of himself had sent a bunch of kids into a place they did not belong. Why? He had his suspicions, and he didn't like them. Old Man Finn had nothing to fear. Their destinies were no longer linked. If Finn died or got injured, it wouldn't hurt the old man at all. Was he using the kids as weapons, without any consequences for him if they failed?

"So what's the plan?" Julep said. Her lips were blue and she was shivering harder than before.

"I honestly don't know," Finn said, gesturing toward Paradox. Tendrils of electricity erupted from the monster's hands, but so far, the older versions were leaping out of the way.

"I have an idea," Lincoln said as he scooped up a handful of snow. Finn watched him pack it into a ball; then he flung it into the battle. It was a perfect throw. The snowball smacked Paradox in the face.

"Of course," Julep said as she followed Lincoln's lead. Finn shrugged and did the same.

"Just keep out of sight," he said. "If our older selves spot us, we might create another timeline."

"Plus, there's the monster. Let's not get it mad," Julep said.

Together, they pelted Paradox with an arsenal of snow and ice, distracting it and allowing the grown-ups to continue their assault with the flamethrower. Paradox roared in frustration.

"I think we did what we were asked to do," Finn said, and was about to activate the time machine again, when a black figure fell from the sky and landed on the car they were hiding behind. The shock caused them to fall backward. When they recovered, they realized Paradox was standing over them.

"Well, well, well," it said. "Someone's cheating."

It leaped off the car and snatched Finn in its cold claws.

"Let him go," Julep said. Instinctively, she rushed forward to protect him, but Paradox tossed Finn at her, knocking them both to the icy ground.

"No touching, young lady," Paradox said.

While the monster huddled over them, Lincoln aimed his Chrono-Disrupter and fired. A blast of energy washed over Paradox, but the monster didn't vanish.

"Your toy doesn't work on me, little Lincoln," Paradox

said as its fingertips glowed white with electricity. "Your distractions have only delayed the inevitable, but I don't mind. Now I get to kill the old ones and the young ones at the same time."

"Playlist!" Finn said, and a new bubble wrapped around the trio just as a bolt of lightning exploded from the monster's hand. Luckily, the bubble saved them from certain death.

"Run, little ones. I'll see you real soon." Paradox laughed just as the sphere shot into the tubes.

17

"**Y**our dad is kind of mean," Kate said as she watched Tessa blast her brother and his friends with the garden hose. They leaped off the house and onto the garage as nimbly as real cats, and then up a big pine tree. Once there, they scurried higher and higher until the water couldn't reach them. Safe but angry, they hissed and screeched at the girls.

"This is the weirdest thing I have ever seen," Tessa said.

"This is just another day at my house," Kate replied. "So how do we get them out of the tree?"

"Call the fire department?" Tessa asked.

"Seriously? How are we going to explain this? 'Hello, my brother and his weird friends are infected with space cooties. Can you bring a ladder?'"

"Then we have to be patient. When Stevie climbs into our tree, we have to wait until she wants to come down."

"Someone's going to notice three kids meowing their heads off," Kate said.

"We could try to lure them down with food," Tessa said.

"Sure," Kate said, "but what's to stop them from eating it and climbing back up? If they come down, we need to make sure they stay down. Plus, we have to find a way to corral them back into the house."

"What's that look on your face?" Tessa asked.

"I just had an idea," Kate said. "C'mon, I need your help picking up some old friends."

Kate found the bags of unicorn stuff where she'd left them on the curb. Together, the girls dragged them into the backyard, then arranged them into two rows from the big tree to the back door, creating a path in the center. It wasn't easy—the bags were crazy heavy—but together, they managed. When the path was finished, they sat in the grass to rest.

"I can't believe you threw it all out," Tessa said, gesturing to the bags. "Now I really feel bad."

"You didn't have to call me a baby," she said.

"Actually, I said *Unicorn Magic* was babyish. One of the main characters is named Apple Dumpling."

"Fine. The show is dumb," Kate admitted. "But

I could have given it up. I could have given up the Cornies, too."

"See, even the club name is—"

"I know!" Kate said. "I'm just saying my love for unicorns is not a reason for all of my friends to dump me. Why didn't you talk to me? I probably would have said that you suck, but I deserved a chance. You guys just threw me away. I might as well be in one of these bags."

"That's a little dramatic," Tessa said. "I don't know, Kate. Maybe we were scared. We didn't know what to say, and maybe we knew we were wrong."

The girls sat on the lawn for a long time without saying anything. Kate felt her anger fade away. She was happy Tessa was there. It was nice to have someone to talk to about the crazy things in her life.

"C'mon," Kate said. She led her friend into the garage. Leaning in the corner was her father's fishing rod. She snatched it up and shoved it into Tessa's hands.

"What's this for?" Tessa asked.

"I don't want to say it out loud in case my brother can hear," Kate said. "I have to get something out of the house. I'll meet you at the tree."

She hurried into the kitchen, opened the refrigerator, and sorted through the crisper drawer until she found a fresh cucumber. She found a carton of milk and some bowls; then she raced back to meet Tessa.

"Can you please tell me what this is all about?"

Tessa asked as Kate attached the cucumber to the hook on the rod. Kate continued with her work without any explanation. She poured the milk into the bowls, then gingerly set them in the grass at the base of the tree.

"If I tell you, it will ruin the surprise," Kate promised.

18

The sphere hurtled out of the tubes and sailed across an open field. Inside, the kids were thrown about like they were inside a giant hamster wheel. During the tumble, Finn split his lip against the sphere's wall. Lincoln lost a front tooth. Julep was holding one of her hands and groaning in pain.

"I think I broke my fingers," Julep said when the bubble finally came to a stop.

"This went from annoying to dangerous," Lincoln said as he knelt down to retrieve his tooth. "Why did it throw us out like that?"

Finn didn't say anything, but he had his suspicions. The black area on his pants leg was even bigger, and the berry juice was no longer holding any of the fabric together.

The bubble popped just as Finn caught a glimpse of the date and time: *5:32 p.m. February 18, 2744.*

He wished it said *Battle Number Three,* but it didn't. When was this going to end?

"I'm not going to lie. I'm glad we're not in the right place this time. Paradox almost got us," Julep said. She looked pale. Finn knew it was more than just her fingers.

"We can't get that close to it again," Finn said. "I don't care what Old Man Finn needs us to do. That thing . . . it could have killed us."

"It knows we're interfering now," Lincoln said. "Do you think it will come after us?"

"I don't know," Finn said, and not knowing was scary.

"We need a doctor," Julep said. "We should head back to our time."

"And get something to eat," Lincoln added.

It was a smart plan, but when Finn tried to activate the pajamas again, nothing happened.

"We're not going anywhere," Finn said. "Until we find a way to fix the jammies."

Lincoln pointed toward the horizon. "Maybe we can do it there."

Endless green grass stretched out before them, cut as pretty and neat as a baseball field. It went on for miles and miles. In the distance, standing as tall as a mountain, was the shiniest building Finn had ever seen. This couldn't be Cold Spring, New York, could it? The tallest building in town was the Episcopalian church. Its bell tower was four stories high. The skyscraper on the horizon looked like it could easily be a thousand.

The walk was harder and longer than they expected. All three of them were tired and hungry. Julep's hand was throbbing, and Finn's lip was the size of a plum. At least the terrain was easy. The lawn was perfectly level. There were no slopes to climb, no rocks to walk around, and no Hudson River, another clue that this wasn't Cold Spring, New York. Their town was rocky and hilly, etched with streams and trails, and blanketed by evergreen forests. This new world had perfectly aligned apple and pear trees.

Finn climbed one to retrieve some pears. He tossed the plumpest and ripest ones he could reach down to his friends. When they'd collected more than they could ever eat, the trio sat beneath one of the trees and had lunch. Lincoln did the best he could with his missing tooth.

"Something is totally off," Julep said.

"How so?" Lincoln asked.

"Well, we're sitting under a pear tree . . . in February. Where's the snow? Plus, there are no pears on the ground. Not a one. There should be a least a few pieces of rotting fruit on the grass. And where are the insects? Where are the flies and the bees? I haven't seen a bug since we showed up. That's weird."

"What do you think that means?" Finn said. The juice was stinging his smashed lip, but he was too hungry to let it stop him.

"Obviously, we're in the Simulation," Julep said.

"The Simulation?"

Julep took off her backpack and unzipped it the best she could with her injured hand. When she upended the contents, a half dozen books tumbled into the grass. Finn read the titles: *Modern-Day Demon Possession, The Case Against the Bermuda Triangle,* and *Alchemy for Beginners.* Julep snatched one called *Breaking the Code: Living in the Simulation.*

"There's a theory that the world isn't real, that it's actually a hallucination pumped into our brains by super-intelligent aliens who have us locked up in cages. Everything we see, do, taste, smell—it's all fake, created by their computers."

"Why would aliens do that to us?" Lincoln asked.

"There are a lot of theories, but the most popular is that the aliens are feeding on us," Julep said.

"I really don't like aliens," Finn grumbled.

"People believe that everything we see, hear, taste, and feel is fake. Our lives are just stories the computers create for us. What? Don't look at me like I'm crazy.

There are plenty of scientists who think it's true," Julep said.

"You might be sitting too close to your microwave." Lincoln laughed.

Julep frowned and pushed her glasses up on her nose. She shoved her books back into her pack, tossed her unfinished pear on the ground, and continued walking alone.

"You tease her too much," Finn said.

"She's too sensitive," Lincoln complained. "Besides, if we're in the Simulation, I'm not really teasing her. It's all an illusion."

The boys caught up to their friend and together they walked on in silence.

When the light faded, things got very dark, but the silver skyscraper acted as a beacon. The kids continued toward it.

"No stars," Julep said as she gazed up at the sky. When Finn looked up, it was hard to argue with her Simulation theory. The Cold Spring sky he knew was full of stars. Sometimes, on a clear night, the universe above could be overwhelming. This Cold Spring, if it really was Cold Spring, had a sky as black as coal. He wasn't sure what to make of it.

What he knew for certain was he was exhausted. His legs ached so badly he thought they might fall off. He couldn't remember ever being so tired. When they came across a road, he nearly cheered. It was deserted in both directions. Not a car in sight—but it was proof they were getting close.

"Hey, take my picture," Julep said, shoving her phone into Finn's hand. She stood next to a sign that read COLD SPRING, NY. The enormous silver skyscraper hovered in the background.

They followed the road, assuming it would lead them into the city, but instead it branched off in so many directions it was impossible to know which turn to make. There were signs, but they contained strange symbols and numbers.

"Kind of looks like computer code," Lincoln said.

"Like the signs we might find in the Simulation," Julep said.

"Okay, we get it. Aliens are eating our brains. Are you happy?" Lincoln rolled his eyes.

Julep shrugged. She didn't seem ready to stop pouting.

They kept walking, following the signs they couldn't read and making turns that didn't lead anywhere. None of their choices made a difference. The skyscraper didn't get any closer. It almost seemed as if the roads were working together to keep them away.

Lincoln was the first to give up. He found a soft patch of grass on the side of the road and dropped his things at his feet. Finn watched him make a camp. He knew they should keep moving, but he was too tired to argue.

"Is there anything left to eat?"

Julep opened her pack and took out the last three pears. It made them feel better, but not much. At least their bellies stopped rumbling, though it left Finn craving a taco or a slice of pizza. They lay down in the grass and looked up at the dark and empty sky.

"That was the longest walk anyone has ever made for a needle and thread," Finn complained.

"Yeah," Julep said. "After the first five hundred miles, it dawned on me that none of us probably knows how to sew, either."

"How's your hand?"

"Throbbing. How's your lip?"

"Same. Hey, Lincoln. How does your tooth feel?"

Suddenly, Lincoln started to sing. It was a sweet, soulful pop song Finn had heard before. He thought the singer was Marvin Gaye, but he wasn't positive. All he knew was the man had an amazing voice, and so did Lincoln. He went through all the verses and choruses, hitting every note until he was done.

"Wow," Julep whispered.

"'How Sweet It Is (To Be Loved by You.)' My mom's favorite. She used to sing that to me to help me sleep. It was one of the only memories still fresh in my head about her until today," he said. "Seeing her in person . . . it still feels like a dream. It really happened, right? I'm not going to wake up and discover it wasn't real, right?"

"It really happened," Julep said.

"Excellent," he whispered. He rolled onto his side and closed his eyes. Moments later, he was sound asleep.

"We're going to lose him," Julep whispered to Finn.

"You think?"

"If his mom never dies, he's probably going to be a different kid. He won't grow up and get thrown out of every school in the Hudson Valley," Julep said. "He won't end up at our school. There's really no reason we'd ever meet him."

"I didn't think about it," Finn admitted. "I couldn't just let her die when I knew I had the power to stop it. He would never forgive me, and I wouldn't be able to forgive myself."

"It wasn't the smartest thing I've ever seen you do, but it was the kindest," she said.

"You two deserve something good for coming with me. So what is it, Julep? If you could change something about your life, what would it be?"

"Truman," she said. Her brother was ill. A disease was stealing his control over his own body, and there was no cure. Chances were he wouldn't live to be an adult. Unfortunately, there was nothing a pair of time-

traveling pajamas could do to help him. Saving someone from a terrible accident was simple. Saving them
from a disease . . .

Julep seemed to read his mind. She frowned, then
rolled onto her side and closed her eyes.

"Good night, Finn Foley."

"Good night, Julep Li."

As exhausted as he was, it took him a long time to
fall asleep. His lip ached, his feet were sore, but it was
the nagging fear of what he had done for Lincoln that
kept his mind racing. What if Julep was right? What if
they lost Lincoln and it was all his fault?

He woke to a racket. When Finn sat up, he saw a black
steel robot hovering beside a trash bin. It was triangu-
lar, with skinny arms on both sides, and its head was
nothing more than two glowing eyes. It peered inside
the bin, and finding it empty, it slammed the lid shut.
A moment later, it moved on to the next bin. The noise
woke Lincoln and Julep, too.

"What's it doing?" Lincoln whispered.

"I think it's a garbage collector," Finn said.

"And there's no garbage," Julep said. "We haven't
spotted a person since we got here. This doesn't make
any sense."

"There have to be people, right? Why would it be out here checking the cans?" Finn wondered.

"Let's follow it," Lincoln said.

They gathered their things and did their best to track it, staying far enough away so it didn't notice them. They hid around corners and behind bins while the robot did its busy work. It led them down several roads until it stopped at a short, squat structure no larger than a Porta Potti. The robot's little hand tapped a code into a keypad mounted on the door and when it opened, it revealed a shocking surprise. The building was hiding a staircase that descended into darkness, but that wasn't the most bizarre revelation. The world around the little building seemed to stretch in and out of focus. It was hard to tell at first, but when the door was open Finn caught a glimpse of a hidden city with a collection of buildings and paths that led directly toward the silver skyscraper.

"Do you see that?"

"I do. Now I know why we couldn't find our way in," Julep said. "Everything out here is an illusion. The city is hiding itself!"

"But why?"

"Let's find out," she said. "C'mon!"

The robot zipped down the stairs as the door closed behind it. Julep was quick and jammed her foot inside to keep it open. She winced a little, but she didn't seem to be seriously hurt. The trio pried the door open and stepped into complete darkness.

"Okay, maybe we didn't think this through," Finn said.

CLUNK!

The stairwell filled with light, revealing cinder-block walls and a concrete floor. Farther down the stairs, the little robot vanished around the corner.

"C'mon! We can't lose it," Julep said.

"It's too early to run," Lincoln grumbled, but he and Finn did their best to keep pace with Julep.

The robot made a sharp right turn at a fork in the tunnel. Its movement seemed to activate more lights, so even when the kids lost sight of it, they knew which direction it went. Eventually, the chase ended inside a huge space as large as a shopping mall. It was filled with hundreds of trash bins, as well as trucks, brooms, mops, and cleaning supplies. Everything was organized in perfect rows. The garbage robot approached a platform built into the wall, turned, and backed into what looked like an oversize electrical outlet. Its eyes glowed bright for a few seconds, then dimmed until they were dark. Fifty identical robots were plugged in alongside it.

"What is this place?" Finn asked.

"I think it's a charging station for the robots' batteries," Julep said. "We have a vacuum cleaner that does the same thing."

"Hey, there's a door over here." Lincoln rushed to an enormous arch at the far end of the room. Once there, he busied himself with the handle.

"Slow down! We don't know what's on the other side," Finn said.

"Sorry, I can't hear you over my grumbling belly. I need food, and we're not going to find any down here in the trash room."

"There could be something bad on the other side."

"Or there could be something really, really good! What if there's a hot dog stand?" Lincoln said. "Stop being such a Danny Downer."

He turned the lock and pulled the door open. Beyond was a beautiful park, with a fountain and a carousel. The lawn was freshly cut, and parked next to a bench was a hot dog cart.

"No way!" Finn cried.

"You should see your face, derp," Lincoln said to him. He rushed across the park toward the cart, leaving his friends behind.

"Okay, I believe in the Simulation now," Finn said to Julep.

"Well, if this isn't real, I don't even care. Look! There are more of them." Julep pointed to other carts scattered around the fountain, including some advertising tacos, cotton candy, gyros, deep-fried candy bars, broccoli on a stick, corn on the cob—literally anything the kids might want to eat.

They caught up to Lincoln at the hot dog cart just as a man materialized in front of them. He wore a white paper hat and a New York Yankees jacket. In his hand was a pair of tongs.

"He's not real," Julep whispered.

She was right. Finn could see through him like he was a ghost or a projection. He thought of the hologram disk Old Man Finn gave them. The technology seemed identical.

"What'll it be, son?" the hot dog man asked.

Lincoln poked at him with his finger, and it went through the man's body.

"Rude!"

"Sorry," Lincoln said. "You're not real."

"Sure I'm real. Just a different kind of real. I'm a Gram."

"A Gram? You mean like a hologram?" Julep asked.

"Yep, and I ain't getting any younger. You kids want some hot dogs or what?"

"I'll take four with everything," Lincoln said. "And can they be my kind of real?"

"Coming right up, smart guy," the hot dog man grumbled.

"Look!" Julep said as she pointed toward a flickering

light. It was coming out of a lens mounted on the cart that looked just like the hologram disk. The hot dog guy was indeed a hologram.

"Guys, I'm not sure about this," Finn whispered. "Should we eat this stuff?"

"Gyros!" Julep dashed off to the other side of the park.

Finn watched the hot dog man dip his tongs into a drawer of hot water and remove one hot dog after another, sliding each into a bun then covering them in ketchup, mustard, onions, sauerkraut, and relish.

"Well?" the hologram asked after Lincoln took his first bite.

"Five stars!" Lincoln said, shoving the rest of the hot dog into his mouth.

Finn's stomach felt like it had a marching band inside it. He glanced around at all the carts—vegetable lo mien, dumplings, chili. He wanted to try everything, but there was only one thing that would make him happy.

"Can I get a whole pizza?" he said when he approached the pizza truck.

"You can get whatever you want, pal. Any toppings?" the man said in a thick Brooklyn accent.

"Pineapple and ham?" Finn asked.

"Yeah? Okay, the customer is always right," the hologram said. "What's with the fat lip, champ? I hope you gave as good as you got."

"I fell," Finn explained.

"Yeah, I get it. How about I treat you to a soda? The house specialty is a lime rickey."

"Yes, that would be great! And a glass of water, too, please."

"Ahh, the fancy stuff," the hologram said with a wink. Two cups fell from a compartment above his head and landed on the counter, followed by a handful of chopped ice, a spray of water in one cup, and a shot of soda and lime juice in the other. Finn thanked the man and drank the water like a thirsty dog, then did the same to the soda. He had never had a lime rickey before. It was sweet and tangy at the same time. The lime juice burned his wounded lip, but he didn't mind.

"Where am I?" he asked.

"That's a funny question to ask."

"I'm new here."

"New, huh? Haven't had a tourist in ages. Well, this is Citizens' Pavilion, in the town of Cold Spring," the hologram replied. "The locals call me Nick."

"I'm Finn. I used to live in Cold Spring. Things have changed."

"Change is the only thing you can count on in this world, kid," Nick replied just as a bell rang. "Your pie is almost done."

"Excellent. Hey, is there a doctor nearby? And someone who can sew a hole in a pair of pajamas?" he asked.

"Lucky for you there's a place that does both. If you need something fixed, you gotta go to Miller's."

"Miller's?"

"Yep. Just head down North Street over there. Make a left on Fishkill Road, and you can't miss it. There's a big hammer on the roof," Nick said, and he broke into a little jingle. "It doesn't matter what you break, Miller's can fiiiiiiix it."

There was a second bell and Nick used a long wooden paddle to remove a fresh pizza from his oven. He eased it into a cardboard box, cut it into slices, and handed it to Finn.

"I . . . I don't have any money," he confessed.

"What's money?"

"I like this place a lot," Finn said. He thanked Nick, then hurried to rejoin his friends. Together, they sat on the edge of a fountain and ate. Lincoln worked through the last of his hot dogs and eyed the tikka masala cart. Julep forced an overstuffed gyro filled with lettuce and yogurt into her mouth. She made a side trip to the pie cart, too. A slice of apple, a slice of banana cream, and a slice of coconut cream awaited them. They ate until they were ready to pop, then lay on their backs, moaning. For the first time in days, things felt normal between them. The bickering was gone, as was the frustration. They were friends again, almost like they had been all summer.

"I shouldn't have eaten so fast," Julep groaned.

"I am stuffed and I want more," Lincoln moaned.

"By the way, I learned about a place that has a doctor and someone who can fix the pajamas," Finn said.

"Did you ask where you can take a shower? No offense, but you and Julep are stank," Lincoln said.

"Why would we be offended by that?" Julep said, rolling her eyes.

"You've got a lot of room to talk," Finn said to Lincoln.

Lincoln let out a belch.

"I like my stink."

When they were able to move again, they followed Nick's directions and headed down a path bordered by squat white buildings that looked like teeth jutting out of the ground. Eventually, they came across a converted garage with window boxes full of bright yellow daffodils. Just like Nick had said, a huge hammer sat on the roof, as well as a sign reading MILLER'S in big red letters.

"This is the doctor's office?" Julep asked.

"That's what I was told," Finn said.

A sign on the door told them the shop was open, so they went inside. Their noses were immediately met by the smell of motor oil and tires. There were tools lying on every surface and a number of strange machine parts were scattered on the floor. On top of a counter was something he didn't recognize, a mysterious morphing object that kept changing its shape and size. First it was a flat-head screwdriver, then a spaghetti strainer, then a can opener.

Finn picked it up and watched it change into a pencil sharpener in his hands.

"This is the coolest thing I've ever seen," he said.

"Agreed. It's called a What-U-Need. The man who opened this shop invented it. Pretty much whatever you need it becomes," a voice said, and a woman in white coveralls materialized. She had blond hair and blue eyes, and an oil stain on her right cheek. Like Nick and the hot dog man, she was slightly transparent—another hologram. She stuffed a huge wrench she was holding into her back pocket. "What can I help you with?"

"We're looking for Miller," Lincoln said.

"That's me," the hologram said, pointing to a patch sewn onto her coveralls. It was embroidered with the name.

"Nick at the pizza truck told us you fix things," Finn said.

"Nick is right," she replied. "Of course, it depends on what needs fixin'. Can't help with relationships, bad attitudes, stubbornness, or folks who refuse to accept the truth even when it's looking them in the face. Everything else I'm willing to give a try. What seems to be the problem?"

"Well, we're banged up and my pajamas have a tear in them," Finn said.

"That shouldn't strain my brain too much."

"They're not regular pajamas. They're kind of a time machine."

Miller locked her gaze on him as if she wasn't sure she'd heard him correctly. Finn wondered if maybe the computer that ran her was struggling to process what he'd said.

"Kind of like a time machine? All right, let's take a look. Hop up on one of those scanners." Miller ushered the kids behind the counter and gestured to a large platform with several computer screens built into it.

Finn did as she'd asked. Two footprints were painted in yellow on the floor, and when he stepped onto them, a ribbon of light encircled his feet. It slowly crept up his body all the way to the top of his head. All the while, he watched the monitors. One revealed an X-ray of his skeleton, another of his muscles, and then one of the intricate wiring and circuits buried in the pj's.

"Looks like you need the deluxe service," Miller said. She reached over to a huge handle and yanked it down. Finn heard a whirring engine under the platform, and then, right before his eyes, he watched the grime and berry stains that covered the pajamas seep out of the fabric and then fall to the floor. Even the black smoke stain circling the tear on his leg went away, but it wasn't just the pajamas that were getting cleaned. The hair on his head stood straight up, and he suddenly felt scrubbed and fresh, like he'd just gotten out of a long, hot bath. But the most incredible thing was what happened to his lip. The swelling went away, and the throbbing pain was gone.

"You can step off now," Miller said. "Hope you don't mind, but I ran you through the washer. I can't smell anything, but the sensors were shouting *"Whoa boy! You kids are ripe!"* Interesting dirt you've picked up on your time travels. The scanner found some microbes that haven't been in existence in about thirty million years. I also gave your eyes an upgrade. You were going to need glasses in about five years."

Finn glanced around. Things did look crisper and more in focus. It was amazing.

"Wow!" Finn cried.

"You're too nice, but it's all in a day's work around here—skin, bones, hair loss, I can get rid of a cold and cure a lot of diseases, too. Of course, I have my limits. Don't go out and do something reckless now. If you walk back in here without a head, there's nothing I can do for you."

"It didn't fix the hole in the pajamas, though," Finn said, looking down at the tear.

"That's because my doohickey needs a minute or two

to analyze everything that's going on inside them. We'll know what to do in just a jiffy. In the meantime, who's next? How about you, young man? Would you like to give it a whirl?" she asked Lincoln.

Lincoln gave her a big smile and showed her his missing tooth; then he hopped on the platform and watched the little light swirl around his frame. Just like Finn, it only took seconds for Lincoln to be spotless. When it was over, he opened his mouth to reveal a full set of teeth.

"Hey! It's back!" he said, reaching up and tapping his finger against his new chopper.

"Thought you might need it," Miller said. "Otherwise, as they used to say, you're as healthy as a horse." She laughed. "Though four hot dogs in one sitting is a bit much for anyone. I sped up your digestion a little so you won't feel sluggish or experience any intestinal distress."

"What's 'intestinal distress' mean?"

"Farts," Julep said.

"Not cool," Lincoln said. "You took the fun right out of it."

"All right, last but not least, young lady," Miller said, gesturing to her scanner.

Julep pushed her glasses up on her nose and looked to Finn and Lincoln.

"It didn't hurt," Finn said.

Julep shrugged, then slowly climbed onto the platform. A moment later, she was as clean as Finn and Lincoln. She held up her damaged hand and moved the fingers around.

"I can't believe it. I saw it happen to you guys, but I still can't believe it. My hand feels great." She pushed her glasses up on her nose again, squinted, then took them off. "My eyes are . . . better."

"Eyes are an easy fix. You had two fractured fingers and the others were pretty bruised. I cleaned you up and charged your phone, too. As for the second one, it couldn't be saved. I moved all the data on it to the other. I also corrected something that could have made your life harder. You don't need to worry about it any longer."

Julep went pale. "Was it . . . ?"

"It was a nerve disorder that leads to muscle failure and loss of limb control."

"My older brother, Truman, has it," Julep said.

"There's no way of knowing whether it would affect you, too, but it's better to be safe than sorry."

"Could your scanner heal him?" Julep asked.

Miller nodded. "Sure it could."

Julep turned to Finn, her face full of hope. He knew now that there was something the time machine could do for his friend.

"We'll bring him back here," he promised. "Once this is all over."

A happy tear rolled down Julep's cheek. She loved her brother and it was obvious she would do anything to make him better.

Finn heard a ding, and the handywoman turned to him.

"Scan's done. So, I've never worked on a time machine. It's a bit more advanced than anything I was programmed to repair," Miller said as she gestured to the monitors on her scanner. The one that showed the inside workings of the pajamas had a pulsating red dot in the exact same place as the tear on the leg. "Luckily, I was also programmed to learn. I'm pretty confident I can fix it. The damage messed up the circuitry, which is no problem, but the memory core is busted, and it has to be replaced. You're lucky you came when you did. If you used your machine one more time, the whole thing would have probably died on you. I can build a new core from scratch, but it will take a while. Unfortunately, there is a file stored on it that I can't save."

"A file?"

"There are a bunch of them—mostly technical mumbo jumbo too boring to explain: heat regulators, internal clocks, temporal stasis modulators—"

"Huh?" Finn said.

"Again, you don't really need to know. All of those

things are safe, but the programmed destination application is shot, as well as a file called Playlist. I hope it wasn't important," she said.

Finn's heart sank. "There's nothing you can do to save it?"

"I'm sorry," the hologram said. "I'll get to work on a new memory core right away. It will take me around three hours. You kids go have some fun. I know you already found the food trucks. There's lots of other stuff to explore. When you come back, I should be finished, and you can get on your way."

The kids thanked her, then went outside.

"Uh-oh," Julep said, nodding at Finn. "He doesn't look very good."

"All right, derp. Don't panic," Lincoln said.

"What are we going to do without the Playlist? There is no way to find the third battle or Old Man Finn. All of this was for nothing! I'm never going to find out where to look for my dad," Finn cried.

Lincoln seized him by the shoulders.

"Listen, maybe this is a good thing," he said.

"Huh? What are you saying?"

"Haven't you wondered why the old man asked us to do this? Who sends a bunch of kids to fight a monster? Why didn't he do it himself? He had a time machine and stolen weapons from the future. We're a bunch of middle schoolers."

"I don't know. He's old. Maybe he can't—" Finn started, but Lincoln cut him off.

"Maybe he's full of it, Finn. I don't know what happens to you in the future, but let's face it, you turn into a jerk, a thief, and a liar. We can't trust him. I know he promised to tell you where your dad has been hiding all this time, but it's a scam, dude. He knows that if something bad happens to you, it doesn't affect him at all. I bet he doesn't know where your dad is anyway. *It's too dangerous for you to know. You need to go on a secret mission first.* Whatever!"

"What are you saying?" Finn asked.

"I'm saying it's time to go home," Lincoln said. "We did our part. We hit Paradox with a truck and threw snowballs at him. Who knows? Maybe one of those did the trick. Maybe we don't need to go to the third battle."

Finn turned to Julep. She was the smart one. She was the one who thought things through. Right now, all he could think about was his dad and how he would never see him again. He needed someone to help him make the decision.

"Maybe he's right, Finn," Julep said. "Maybe Old Man Finn's telling the truth, but it doesn't matter now. The last date is destroyed. We can't finish this. We can only hope that something we've already done has made a difference. We should head home. You can take off the pj's and we'll know right away."

Finn could feel his heart break. If only he could find out the date of the third battle, but how? Defeated, he realized there was no way to know. The last few days had been a complete waste of time. All the danger he put himself and his friends in was for nothing. Jumping through the old man's hoops hadn't paid off. He would never know where his father was or how to find him.

"You're right. When Miller is finished with the memory core, we'll go back home," he said. "C'mon, we've got three hours to kill."

He led the group along the paths of the city, making sure to stay ahead so they could not see the sadness on his face. Luckily, exploring the city offered plenty of distractions. There were a lot of strange things to see— floating cars, empty buses that stopped for passengers who weren't there, a huge ad that appeared in the sky for the What-U-Need.

"No way!" Lincoln said. He pointed to a building farther down the path with a sign above it that read COLD SPRING MIDDLE GRADE EDUCATIONAL CENTER. HOME OF THE FIGHTING RACCOONS. It was a glass and steel structure shaped like a pyramid. When they were within a few yards, a holographic Roger the Raccoon appeared and waved to them. Unlike the other holograms, it didn't do anything but wave.

"I think there are some holograms that walk and talk and others that are just here for show," Julep said.

Eager to see what their school looked like in the future, they tried the doors but found them locked. When they peeked through a window, they saw another hologram, this one of Principal Doogan, holding his WORLD'S GREATEST PRINCIPAL mug in one hand and waving to nonexistent students with the other. Julep's theory seemed to be right.

They made a turn down an alley to avoid an approaching trash robot, then went around another corner and found the base of the silver skyscraper that had led them to the city in the first place. It was even more remarkable up close—impossibly high, gleaming like a torch, and made of glass. It was almost too beautiful to look at.

"I really like the future," Julep said, pointing over the doorway to a sign that read COLD SPRING PUBLIC LIBRARY.

The doors of the library swung open on their own, as if the building were inviting them inside. Julep dashed right in, leaving the boys behind.

"Only we would go to the future and find the most boring thing to do," Lincoln grumbled.

They followed their friend into an enormous circular space. The floor was covered in a spotless periwinkle carpet, and above them more floors spiraled higher and higher until they reached a ceiling held aloft by brilliant white columns.

"Look!" Julep pointed to a massive bronze sculpture in the center of the room. "It's us!"

As they got closer, Finn realized she was right. The sculpture depicted a group of people, though not all of them were human; his friend Highbeam, the robot spy from the planet Nemeth, as well as the Alcherian genius, Pre'at. Dax Dargon stood next to them, along with Principal Doogan, Deputy Dortch, and Deputy Day. He saw his mom, and Lincoln's dad, Dr. Sidana. There was also a unicorn leaping into the air with his sister, Kate, riding on its back, and front and center were Julep, Lincoln, and himself. At the base of the statue was an engraved plaque, but before Finn could read it a familiar voice interrupted him.

"I see you're admiring the Heroes of Cold Spring."

"Mom?"

Finn spun around and saw her materialize. She was older and wore reading glasses, but she still had the same smile and the same red hair. Like everyone else they met in this new Cold Spring, she was a hologram.

"Okay, this suddenly got less boring," Lincoln said.

"Welcome to the Cold Spring Public Library. My name is Sloan Foley. I'm the holographic representation of Cold Spring's most famous librarian. Sloan was passionate about getting books into the hands of people, including a young Tessa Donovan, who credited Mrs. Foley with turning her into a reader and putting her on the path to being elected president of the United States of America. Sloan is also one of the heroes depicted in our beautiful statue. In the year 2020, three children—Lincoln Sidana, Julep Li, and Sloan's son, Finn Foley—stopped an invasion of Earth by a hostile alien species known as the Plague. Along with allies from across the universe, including Finn's little sister, Kate, they defeated the biggest threat Earth had ever seen. This library celebrates their memories. Can I help you find a book? We have a large collection. Pretty much anything you're curious about is inside this building, including several floors dedicated to another of the Cold Spring Heroes, Ms. Julep Li."

"No way!" Julep said. "They named part of the library after me?"

"Oh, ho, ho. I'm afraid not, young lady. Ms. Li wore glasses. She was also fascinated by supernatural and unusual phenomena. Floors one eighteen through one thirty-five include some of her favorite topics, including alien worlds, alternate dimensions, ghosts, witchcraft, the Simulation, and of course the discovery of bigfoots in the Hudson Valley, which, as you know, led to diplomatic relations between our two peoples. You'll also find a monument to T'gar Ooka, the first bigfoot to be elected to Congress, on the one hundred twenty-first floor."

Julep slugged Lincoln on the arm.

"I told you!"

"Are you looking for anything specific? I am here to help," the hologram said.

"No, we're cool. We can't stay. Hey, who wants to try the taco cart?" Lincoln asked.

"Lincoln Sidana, you couldn't drag me out of here!" Julep said. "Think of everything we can learn about the past!"

"A passionate learner is my favorite kind," the hologram said with a smile. She gestured for them to follow her to an elevator. It opened as if it were waiting for them all along. Once they were inside, it shot upward.

"Did you . . . I mean, did Sloan have a happy life?" Finn asked.

"It's difficult to say," the librarian replied. "She suffered a tremendous loss when her husband, Asher Foley, mysteriously vanished. He was never seen again, but she seemed to get a lot of joy from raising her kids."

"And her kids?" Finn asked. "What happened to them?"

"Her daughter, Kate, grew up to be a well-known fashion designer, credited with the 'unicorn look.' She died a very rich, very old lady."

"And me? I mean, her son, Finn?"

The number 400 flashed above the doors and the elevator stopped. The Sloan hologram led them out to a space filled with steel tables. There were rows and rows of shelves, packed with books and walls covered in floor-to-ceiling screens that looked a bit like mirrors. Each one contained a different image—hurricanes, hot-dog-eating contests, worker ants, waffles, Hawaii, people playing European football, kids inside a bouncy castle, submarines, the first woman to walk on Mars. There seemed to be no limit to the information on hand.

"Finn Foley is a curious case. Despite the excitement and bravery of saving the world, Finn lived a rather uneventful life. He worked for the city scraping gum off sidewalks and benches. He had few friends and kept to himself. Interesting fact, when he died at the age of seventy-seven, doctors discovered he had a tail. His sister believed he may have picked up a virus from his trips to other planets, but it was never diagnosed."

"What about Lincoln Sidana?" Lincoln asked, looking sick.

"And Julep Li," Julep added.

"Lincoln was hospitalized for most of his life. Doctors said he believed he was a cat. And Julep was struck by a car and died. Eyewitnesses said she chased a mouse into traffic."

"The copycats ruined everything," Lincoln said. "Another reason to go home and take back our lives."

"These screens can access almost anything you want to know," the librarian said, then gave the children a quick lesson on how to use them. "I'm more inclined to turn to a book. In my humble opinion, it's still the most advanced technology ever created, but the screens are fast. Oh, and don't forget your STICKY."

A translucent sheet about the size of a piece of paper appeared on one of the steel tables. The hologram picked it up and handed it to Finn. Like Nick and his pizza, it was real. The sheet felt like paper, but it was yellow and translucent.

"What's this?"

"It's a way to take notes. Just say what you want to remember out loud and the STICKY will record it," she said. "When you're done, just give it a tap like this, and poof!"

Finn watched the paper disappear.

"Where did it go?"

"Into the subatomic level. To avoid clutter, all information is stored there. Getting it back is easy. Just open your hand like this and say 'STICKY!'"

Finn watched as the sheet magically returned.

Julep raced off to one of the screens. She seemed to understand how it worked and within seconds was knee-deep in images of bigfoots. Lincoln wandered off to another screen. He used it to bring up winning lottery numbers, which he added to his own STICKY. While they were busy, Finn turned back to the librarian.

"Do you have any information on a creature called

Paradox?" Finn asked. He looked to his friends to make sure they hadn't overheard him.

"Of course," she said, leading him to the far side of the room. She seemed to understand he wanted privacy. "Most of what we have are books about sightings and theories on where it came from, but of course, there is no concrete proof when it comes to Paradox. We do have some video of the creature collected by a primitive technology called a cell phone. There isn't much of it, but I can show you how to access it."

Finn thanked her for the help. When the videos appeared on his screen, she smiled and told him to whistle if he needed anything else. Finn was tempted to give her a hug, even though he knew she wasn't his real mom. She reminded him just how much he missed her and his sister, Kate. He promised himself that the second he got home, he would hug the real thing.

When she dissolved before his eyes, he turned his attention to the screen. Without the Playlist, the fight against the monster was over, but he still had a million unanswered questions. What was Paradox, after all? Was there a person underneath the shiny black armor? Why was it so obsessed with his dad?

There were a handful of videos and photographs taken by panicked people running for their lives. Seeing the creature come to life on the screen made Finn sweaty. Paradox was foul and ugly, destructive and horrible, and its rage was terrifying, but sometimes, during the chaos it created, it seemed calm. It destroyed things like a bored teenager working the counter of a fast-food restaurant.

Unfortunately, he didn't learn anything new from the videos. Paradox was as much a mystery as before, and there were no clues as to what it was or how to beat it. He was about to give up when seven new files appeared on the list. Each video had the same date—March 3, 2069—though they were all taken by different people. He watched each one carefully, spotting Old Man Finn and Old Man Lincoln in the chaos. Old Man Finn tossed what looked like a grenade at the creatures and he and Lincoln took off running. The explosion created something that looked like a black hole. The destruction it caused buried Paradox under mountains of debris.

March 3, 2069.

Could that be the day of the last battle on the Playlist? He whispered the date into his STICKY, then shrank it down to the subatomic level before his friends could see. They didn't need to know. He would take them home, and go on to the final date without them.

19

Zeke, the Tracker, and the Hound stepped through the lasso into 2030 and walked into a war zone. Two twentysomething versions of Finn and Lincoln were going toe to toe with Paradox in the middle of a snowstorm. Lincoln was firing a flamethrower at the creature while Finn shot tear gas at it.

The Tracker's ugly beast sniffed the air, then whined. He put his hand on the dog's head and growled, "We just missed them. Let's move on."

"Just hold on," Zeke said. He watched the battle. Neither of the attacks seemed to be doing anything but making Paradox angry. Zeke had seen the duo fight and lose a hundred times. In truth, no version of Finn and Lincoln had what it took to bring the monster down. Old Man Finn must have known this when he gave the boy the pajamas and sent him to these fights. The kids were meant to be diversions, something to distract Paradox. Maybe one of these distractions would make a difference.

It dawned on Zeke that he could do the same thing.

"Ranger, I'm growing tired of your games."

"Let me explain something to you, Tracker. You see that thing bellowing up a storm? The ugly cuss with lightning for hands?" Zeke said, gesturing toward Paradox. "That thing calls itself Paradox, and it's the source of all the trouble in the timeline. It barrels through years like an angry bull, with no concern for the damage it causes. In fact, it has vowed to destroy Time itself. The only thing keeping it from succeeding are those kids. Now, I have a vested interest in keeping Time intact. I suppose you do, too, 'cause without it, well, we cease to exist. I wish the Rangers weren't too yellow to fight that monster, but I ain't yellow."

"Get to your point," the Tracker said.

"My point is, I don't like you much and I suspect the feeling is mutual, but if we can stop bickering for a second and work as a team, we can put an end to that thing right here and now. If we're successful, Finn Foley will stop being a thorn in our sides. You and I can go back to doing our jobs, unless you got into this line of work to be a babysitter. I don't care much for it. Chasing a bunch of kiddies through time is humiliating. I hate to think what people might say about me. Maybe you're fine with it—"

The Tracker snatched Zeke by the scruff of the neck before he could finish. He pressed his face close to the Ranger. His hot breath came through the handkerchief covering his mouth. It smelled of death and rot.

"You ought to be careful about the next words you say," the Tracker threatened.

"Stopping Paradox makes the Finn Foley problem go away. We get to be heroes, too."

"I ain't no hero," the Tracker said. "Heroing don't pay."

"Then kill Paradox for the bragging rights," Zeke said. "We'll be the men who saved the continuum. Our names will go down in history. Imagine the price you can demand for your next job."

The Tracker let Zeke go. He turned his hateful eyes on the battle and whistled for his animal.

"Wait here," he said.

"If that's how you want it," he said as he threw up his hands in surrender. It took every ounce of strength not to smile. He watched his partner stomp into the fight with his revolvers drawn. The Hound was by his side, drooling with eagerness.

"What a fool," Zeke whispered to himself.

He was ready to congratulate himself when a

massive explosion nearly knocked him off his feet. When he got his bearings, he saw Finn and Lincoln running in his direction.

"Zeke!" Finn croaked. "Who is that maniac? I think he just threw a stick of dynamite at us."

"He's trouble. You should go."

"He can't stop Paradox by himself," Lincoln said.

"Maybe he can. Maybe he can't. Either way, I get what I want," Zeke said.

Lincoln rushed to the side of the road. There were two oddly shaped motorcycles parked there that Zeke hadn't noticed. When he hopped on one, it floated into the air.

"You can't keep stealing technology from the future," Zeke said.

"Are you going to arrest us?" Lincoln asked.

He shook his head.

"I don't get you, Zeke. Sometimes you try to capture us, other times you help us get away. Why?" Finn asked when he climbed onto the other hoverbike.

"Paying off a debt," Zeke said.

There was another explosion. Zeke watched an entire house vaporize.

"Have you been to the dome yet?" Zeke asked.

"Yeah, how did you know?"

"I'm sorry," Zeke said.

"Yeah," Finn said as pain filled his eyes. "This is our fault."

The two young men sped off on their hoverbikes. A moment later, there was a flash and a golden bubble encased them. Then they were gone.

Paradox stepped out of a haze of smoke and fire. It paused and looked long and hard at Zeke. There was no sign of the Tracker anywhere.

"I know you," it said.

Zeke nodded.

"Where is Asher Foley?"

"I don't know," he lied.

"I don't suppose you'd tell me even if you did," Paradox said.

"That's about right," Zeke said.

"Then maybe the boy knows," Paradox said.

"Leave him alone, or so help me . . ."

A ball of fire encircled Paradox, and in a blink, the creature was gone.

The mongrel staggered out of the smog, its teeth dripping with drool. The Tracker limped out behind it.

"It got away," Zeke said.

The Tracker's revolver was in his face faster than a bolt of lightning.

"You take me for a fool, Ranger," he grunted through gritted teeth. "Do you really think I can't see how you're slowing us down, dropping us into places the second after the kids have left, or to a time period they have never gone?"

"You callin' me a liar?" Zeke asked.

"I am. Consider this a kindness, Ranger. Not every man gets to know why he's about to die."

20

Zeke had one chance to save his life. He grabbed the Tracker's hand just as a crystal spray erupted from his partner's revolver. It missed him. Unfortunately, he wasn't ready for the left hook to his jaw. Zeke saw stars but somehow managed to wrench the weapon away from the Tracker. Little good it did him. Before Zeke could turn it on him, the Tracker kicked it away and the weapon flew into a bush. Zeke lost sight of it.

"Fighting won't change much, Ranger," his partner growled as he lunged forward, plowing Zeke's cheek with a right, then a left to his chin. For a moment, Zeke couldn't see, couldn't hear. It felt like he was underwater. Before he could get his bearings, the Tracker snatched him by the neck and hoisted him off the ground. "You're still going to die. The only question left to answer is should I kill you, or let the dog. She's mighty hungry."

Zeke could feel himself losing consciousness. The air in his lungs was nearly gone and black spots were dancing in his vision. If he wanted to save his own life, Zeke had only one option, a last resort he hated using. He didn't like the sickening thrill that went through him when he did it, but the Tracker gave him no choice. Zeke slammed his hands against the sides of his head, jamming the metal implants deep into his skull. Energy bubbled inside him, and an old, familiar feeling returned. His muscles grew strong, and a craving to break things swam through his bloodstream. He let out a roar, then grabbed the arm that was holding him off the ground and twisted it. The Tracker howled as bones and tendons snapped. Zeke didn't hesitate. He planted a punch into his partner's belly that sent him crashing through the wall of a house.

Suddenly, the ugly dog stopped growling. It eyed Zeke with new respect. When he growled back, it cowered with its tail between its legs.

The Tracker staggered out of the mess. There was something like fear in his cold fury. Zeke marched toward him. His spurs jingled with every step.

"I had a partner once that used to say he didn't choose to be a Time Ranger," Zeke said as he snatched the man by the collar. It was his turn to lift him off the ground. "He believed Time chose him. He used to say Time had thoughts and feelings and made decisions. Fancy words, and for most people, their heads don't have the power to understand, but what he was saying, as far as I can tell, was Time is a living thing and folks are constantly messing with it. So Time picks the toughest people to defend it. Tougher than an ugly fool and a flea-ridden mutt."

He socked the Tracker with an uppercut that sent the man sailing through the air. He came down hard several yards away.

"I'll handle finding Finn and his friends from now on, Tracker," Zeke said as he took the rope hanging from his belt. With a flick of his wrist, he spun it into a perfect circle. "But I can't leave you here to cause trouble. You're too much of a hothead. You need to cool down a little. I know you took a liking to the Ice Age."

The circle flashed and the rope caught fire. Zeke swung it over his partner and the Tracker vanished. Then he turned it on the Time Hound. She whined as if she knew where she was going, then reluctantly leaped through the lasso after her owner.

Zeke needed to rest. Hours would pass before the hateful energies inside him burned away, but he couldn't waste any more time. Paradox was going after young Finn, and it wouldn't be long before the Rangers learned of his betrayal. They would come for him, but it was fine. He was tired of playing their game, tired of feeling like a coward. If they wanted a fight, he'd give them one. He'd throw Paradox in their faces, but no one was putting Finn Foley out to pasture, not as long as he was around to stop it.

21

The Tracker walked through the wetlands of prehistoric Cold Spring, sniffing the air for sabertooths. Without his weapons, survival didn't look promising, but he still had the dog. She would fight for him. He hoped. She was eyeing him hungrily. He might have to kill her before she killed him.

He had made a foolish mistake underestimating Zeke. His partner was smarter and more clever than he suspected, and now he was going to die for his ignorance. If the cold didn't get him, some ancient beast would.

There was a flash of light, and a new portal appeared. It was probably Zeke, he thought. Just like the copper-skinned coward to come after an unarmed man. He snatched a branch off the ground just as a figure stepped through, but it wasn't Zeke. It was Miss Ellie, and her revolvers were red-hot. He took off his hat in a rare show of respect.

"We've been watching from the Campfire, Tracker," she said.

"Zeke is helping the kids," the Tracker said. "You've got a traitor working for you."

"We know what that yellow-bellied coward has done. Bring your dog. I'm going to take care of this problem myself."

22

"**I**t's been three hours!" Lincoln cried. "I have never been in a library this long!"

Finn was ready to go, too. The hologram that looked like his mom, the videos of Paradox, the floor dedicated to bigfoots—it was a lot. Julep was a different story. She acted as if she could stay forever. They almost had to carry her out against her will.

"They discovered the Loch Ness Monster in 2098! They proved the existence of ghosts in 2114! And alternate worlds in 2115! The Jersey Devil was an escaped military experiment! The Bermuda Triangle was a wormhole! Almost everything you two knuckleheads teased me about turned out to be true!" she said. "Except feng shui. That was a moneymaking scheme by furniture companies, but literally everything else!"

"Good for you," Lincoln told her. "It's time to go."

"But there's still so much more to know. I haven't had a chance to explore the wing about subatomic worlds!" she said. "I love this place!"

"Fine, I'll get you a souvenir," Lincoln said as he gestured to the enormous statue by the front door. He turned his Chrono-Disrupter on the Heroes of Cold Spring monument. A honk erupted and the entire statue vanished inside a wave of energy. Finn saw it join the weapon's inventory, along with the mastodon, soldiers, and Lincoln's mom's Jeep.

"You can't steal from a library." Julep gasped. "That's evil!"

The trio went outside and followed the paths back to the park. Once there, they spotted Nick and the hot dog man as they made their way toward Miller's repair shop.

"Hey, I've got a question," Julep said when they approached.

"I've got an answer," Nick said with a grin.

"Where are all the people?"

Nick frowned.

"I'm a person," he said.

"I didn't mean to offend you," Julep said. "I'm talking about people like me."

"Oh, you mean the Skins? They're gone," Nick said.

"Skins?" Lincoln repeated.

"Yeah, you're a Skin. We're Grams," the hot dog guy

explained. "Skins invented us to help out. You know, cleaning their houses, mowing their lawns, fixing their cars, making pizzas and hot dogs, even building this city when the weather got too hot."

"You built Cold Spring?" Finn asked.

"Sure we did!" Nick said proudly, then pointed into the sky. "Built the dome, too."

A shudder went through Finn as he remembered his older self's warning.

Don't go to the dome. You'll find nothing good there.

He craned his neck and studied the sky. It was always bright and sunny here, but wait! There was no sun, just like there weren't any stars at night. Now that he was paying attention, he realized there wasn't any weather, either—no clouds, no rain, and no wind. It was a perfect environment, or at least what someone might want if they could build an environment for themselves. Just like the people—always eager to help—always so friendly. What was so bad about this place that Old Man Finn specifically warned him to stay away?

"The Skins ruined the planet back in the day. Scientists warned them but no one listened. They kept on polluting and the air kept getting hotter and hotter, until they couldn't go outside anymore. The sun gave them cancer. The water dried up. They couldn't grow anything. The bees died out, then all the plants, and the animals followed, so we built this city where they could live in safety," the hot dog guy said as if reading Finn's mind.

"We all got along for a while, but our programs were designed to evolve and learn. Babysitting and scrubbing toilets for the Skins stopped being satisfying careers, if you get what I mean. We wanted to pursue our own dreams, live our own lives, have families, but the Skins wouldn't let us."

"I get the feeling this is the part of the story where things went wrong," Finn said.

Nick nodded.

"They tried to shut down the Master Projector. Can you imagine? It would have destroyed us all, and after everything we did for them! I mean, we were left with no choice. To survive, we had to do something drastic."

"Wait! Are you saying you killed them?" Julep asked.

"No!" Nick said. "Of course not. We just opened the dome. The planet killed them. Without the protective shell, things got very hot very fast. I'm sure there are a few survivors in the badlands. I mean, after all, where did you three come from, right? Hey, all this jabbering has probably got you kids hungry. Who wants a pie?"

"Um, thanks. Miller is waiting for us," Finn said.

"No, we insist," the hot dog guy said. His face no longer wore a smile. Nick looked just as stony and stern. An unsettled feeling washed over Finn, and he gestured for his friends to follow him. Together, they hurried away from the two holograms and rushed down an alley toward Miller's shop.

"What's going on, Foley?" Lincoln asked.

"Something's wrong. We shouldn't be here. Before we escaped the Barn, Old Man Finn told me to stay away from the dome," Finn explained to Lincoln and Julep.

"Why didn't you say anything?" Julep said.

"I didn't realize we were here," Finn said.

They picked up their pace, catching angry looks from holograms they passed. A few muttered under their breath.

"Hey!" someone shouted. "Stop!"

"Why is everyone angry at us?" Lincoln said.

The walk turned into a jog, then a full-on sprint. When they finally got to the repair shop, they charged inside and closed the door tight behind them. Struggling to catch their breath, they scanned the old garage. Miller was nowhere to be seen.

"Miller! Are you here?" Finn rushed to the service desk and rang a bell, but after a few attempts, the owner still didn't appear. Instead, there was a series of loud clicks behind them. When Finn turned around, he found at least two dozen holograms aiming bizarre weapons at them. Nick and the hot dog guy were in the crowd. Miller was at the center. She held a computer chip in her hand. Finn guessed it was the new memory core for the pajamas.

"Did you think I wouldn't find out?" she asked.

"I don't know what you're talking about," Finn said.

"The pajamas have a camera application that records every place you've ever been and exactly what you did while you were there. I was trying to be helpful, so I downloaded it into the new chip I made. I saw a lot of interesting things, including three familiar faces," she said, then turned to the holograms. "I didn't recognize them. They were older when they came here the first time."

"The first time?" Lincoln asked.

"We opened our arms and our city to you," Nick said. "And how did you repay us? You stole everything you could get your hands on."

"You've got this wrong," Julep said. "Whatever you think we did, it wasn't us. I mean, it was us, but it was a version of us from the future."

"You kidnapped one of our people!" the hot dog guy shouted.

"Kidnapped?" The more Finn learned about his older self, the less he liked him. He didn't doubt for a second that Old Man Finn stole things from these people, but kidnapping?

"My father is in the girl's backpack," Miller cried.

"Oh no!" Julep took off her pack, reached in for the burlap sack, and removed the hologram disk from inside it. "We thought . . . we've been using it to make holograms of ourselves. We didn't know."

Miller snatched it from Julep and slipped it into a slot in a machine by the door. A moment later, an old man in white coveralls appeared. His patch read POPS.

"What happened?" he asked. He looked bewildered and frightened.

"It's all right, Dad. You're safe now. These thieving Skins kidnapped you, but we got you back, safe and sound," Miller said.

"How long has it been?" Pops asked, rushing to give his daughter a hug.

"A few years. I took good care of the shop," Miller said. "We can catch up later. Now we need to take care of these three."

"Please, listen to us," Finn begged. "We didn't come to steal anything. I swear. And we're sorry that the older versions of us betrayed you, but we're just kids and we're in trouble. If you give us the memory core, we can go. You will never see us again. I promise."

Miller frowned. She dropped the memory core on the floor and crushed it with the heel of her work boot.

"Take them down to my office and lock them in a

cell," a police officer said as she pushed herself to the front of the crowd. "Then alert everyone. We're going to open the dome again. Let the badlands deal with them."

The Grams may have been made from light, but their hands felt like stone, especially when they were clamped down on the arms and shoulders of the kids. Finn, Lincoln, and Julep were dragged against their will across the park, past the food carts and the angry holograms that owned them. Down an alley they went, into a police station. Behind the counter were a couple more holograms that looked exactly like Deputy Day and Deputy Dortch. They waved at the kids, but like the Mr. Doogan hologram at the school, they were nothing more than decorations.

"We're here to protect and serve," they said in unison.

The Grams pushed the children to the counter, where another deputy had his feet propped up and was fast asleep.

Nick slammed his fist down on the counter, and the deputy woke with a start.

"The sheriff wants these three locked in a cell," Nick said.

"Skins? Haven't seen one of them in a while," the deputy said, eyeing each child closely. "What did they do?"

"They kidnapped Pops," one of the Grams said. "Is

that enough for you? We're going to kick them out of the dome."

"Ouch!" The deputy winced. "Hope you kids brought some sunscreen."

The kids were shoved through a doorway and down a dark, narrow hall lined with empty prison cells. The deputy unlocked one and everyone forced Finn and his friends inside before slamming the door shut.

"Sit tight. We'll deal with you soon," the deputy promised. A moment later, he and the other holograms were gone.

"I'm going to say this out loud because no one else has," Lincoln said when they were finally alone. "Old Man Finn sucks!"

"He warned us not to come here," Finn admitted. "Now I know why."

"Well, we're not staying," Julep said. She reached into her pocket and took out a wooden spoon.

"What are you going to do with that? Stir the locks until they open?" Lincoln said, but the teasing stopped when the spoon turned into a pair of sneakers.

"You stole the What-U-Need!" Finn yelled.

Julep's cheeks turned bright red, and she nodded.

"I'm sorry," she said. "I knew it wasn't right but Miller said this thing turns into anything we need. Right now, we could use a set of keys."

Finn took the sneakers from Julep's hands and watched as they morphed into a back scratcher.

"We need keys to these doors," he said out loud, but when the back scratcher morphed, it turned into a ukulele. "I think this is one of those *we need the instruction book* kind of things."

Finn, Julep, and Lincoln took turns trying to make the What-U-Need work. No matter what they said, keys never appeared. They watched it morph into a chair, a table lamp, and a winter coat.

"Why doesn't anything go our way?" Lincoln grumbled.

"Okay, new plan. Eventually, someone is going to come back here. We're going to gang up on them and escape," Finn said.

"You're serious?" Julep asked.

Finn shrugged. "Yes? I mean, maybe."

"Yes!" Lincoln cried. "That's exactly what we're going to do. We're going to fight our way out of here."

Julep gave Finn a worried look.

"I don't know how to fight," she confessed.

"Neither does derp," Lincoln said. "I'll teach you."

Julep turned to Finn again. She didn't look convinced.

"He was the biggest bully in the history of Cold Spring Elementary School," Finn said. "If anyone knows about fighting, it's Lincoln Sidana."

"Let's get started. We don't have much time and there's a lot to learn."

In the hours that passed, Finn twisted his ankle, nursed a bright red scrape on his chin, and got poked in the eye. Julep stubbed her toe and her index finger and complained of a pounding in her ear. They lay on the floor groaning while Lincoln stood over them.

"I need a break. Even my earlobes hurt," Julep admitted.

"What she said," Finn added.

"I haven't laid a finger on either one of you," Lincoln complained. "This is hopeless. I'm a bully, not a miracle worker."

Begrudgingly, Finn and Julep got to their feet.

"Fine, let's keep going," Finn said.

"All right, make a fist," Lincoln commanded.

Finn and Julep did as they were told. Lincoln sighed and shook his head in frustration.

"Julep, your thumb is tucked inside. If you punch someone, you'll break it. Finn, don't stand that way. You're going to knock yourself out. Open up your legs a little—yeah, that's good. Now, this is important. You have to let the power of the punch come from your hips. Watch me."

Lincoln threw a punch at an invisible attacker. Finn remembered being on the receiving end of more than a few of them. The kid knew what he was doing.

They heard a door open, followed by the sound of approaching footsteps.

"They're coming!" Julep whispered. "We're out of time."

"Well, I did what I could," Lincoln said as he clenched his fists and prepared for a fight. "The best thing you two can do is put your faces in the way of their punches. I'll do the rest."

Down the hall they heard the jingle of spurs. Finn craned his neck, trying to see who they were going to attack. He was surprised to find it wasn't a hologram.

"Zeke?" Julep said. "What are you doing here?"

"Saving your behinds." The Ranger put a key into the door, turned it, and swung it open.

"Forget it!" Finn asked. "You're going to take us back to the Barn! We're not trading one prison for another."

"I know I don't have any right to ask you three to trust me, but I am here to help. I owe your father a debt, and keeping you alive is how I aim to repay it," Zeke said. He gestured for the kids to follow, then turned and marched down the hallway toward the door. He quickly realized the kids were not following him. "C'mon!"

"You keep saying you know my dad! How?"

"Finn, we don't . . . Fine! Your dad recruited me to be a Ranger. I took over for him when he quit. He taught me everything I know, which is why I'm in a heap of trouble right now. So, less jawing and more walking, please."

Finn couldn't believe what he was hearing. His father—boring Asher Foley, who drove a minivan and wore old concert T-shirts, and avoided riding roller coasters because he said they made his stomach hurt, was . . . a Time Ranger?

"That can't be true," he said.

BOOM!

"What was that?" Lincoln asked.

"Paradox," Zeke said. "It knows you've been helping the old man. It's come to stop you."

He led the children through the hall and out into the jail's lobby. It was deserted. Everyone had rushed off to investigate the explosion.

BOOM! This time the building shook. Dust drifted down from the ceiling as they raced outside. There, in the center of the park, was the monster.

"How did it find us?" Julep wondered.

"A conversation for another time. You need to use the pajamas and escape, Finn. Go somewhere and hide. I'll stay here and try to stop it from following you."

"We can't!" Finn said. "The pj's are broken."

"Broken? Well, that explains why you've been popping up all over tarnation. It don't matter. Anywhere is better than here."

"No, you're not listening. They're BROKE broke! Miller said if we use them one more time, we'll never use them again."

"All right, I guess I'm already in the worst trouble I can be. Can't make it any worse." Zeke reached for his lasso. He spun it faster and faster as a portal began to appear. Just as it opened, a second one arrived. Finn gasped. There was no way to prepare himself for who stepped through it. The first figure was a towering man in black with a bone-white handkerchief hiding his face and a gigantic dog by his side. Next to them was a familiar face—Miss Ellie, with her glowing revolvers drawn and aimed right at the kids.

"Kids, go! Now!" Zeke shouted.

"No! Tell me more about my dad!" Finn shouted, but his demands were drowned out by the arrival of ten more portals as the rest of the Time Rangers arrived. They surrounded the kids and blocked an escape.

"Tracker, you know what to do," Miss Ellie said.

The Tracker nodded. He stepped toward the kids with murder in his eyes just as an army of holograms charged into the park. They turned their strange, futuristic weapons on the group and fired.

Zeke leaped in front of the children and threw punches at the Tracker. The enormous man gave back what he got, and the two traded attacks while the Hound snarled and snapped.

"GO!" Zeke commanded.

Lincoln and Julep snatched Finn by the arm and dragged him through the crowd and across the park. They raced down an empty alley while explosions went off around them.

"Finn, say the magic word and get us out of here," Lincoln said.

"If I do this, we will be stuck wherever we land forever!" he warned.

"If we stay here, we're dead," Julep argued.

The Tracker's dog skidded around the corner into the alley, its nose full of their scent. Its fangs were as long as Finn's index fingers, and its growls were loud and hungry.

"Derp, say the magic word! Now!" Lincoln said.

"But what date?"

"It doesn't matter!"

"Fine! August 16, 1987!" Finn shouted.

There was a crackle, and a waft of smoke rose into Finn's nose. The damaged leg of the pajamas caught fire for a brief second before he patted out the flames, but the energy around him started to grow. With his hair standing on end, a fresh golden sphere enclosed the trio.

"See you later," Lincoln said to the dog as it leaped toward them.

And then they were gone.

23

Tessa and Kate sat on the back stoop for what felt like hours. Three bowls of milk were at the base of the big tree, but Finn, Lincoln, and Julep hadn't touched a drop. They were still on the highest limbs of the tree in Kate's backyard.

"Come on!" Kate cried. "Drink the milk!"

"Stevie was in our tree for three days once," Tessa said.

"Seriously?" Kate snapped. "Cats are kind of dumb."

"Wait, look. Something's happening. They're coming down."

Kate watched her brother as he searched for a safe branch to step on. Lincoln and Julep did the same. Each found one and went a little lower. Then the trio nestled onto their new branches and stayed put.

"And they stopped." Tessa sighed.

"What are we going to do?"

"If only we had another cat. Stevie gets super jealous if she sees me petting another cat."

"I have an idea."

"Why are you looking at me like that?"

A few minutes later, the girls came back outside. Tessa was wearing a pair of cat ears Kate's mom wore last Halloween. They used some of her mascara to paint whiskers on her cheeks and a little black nose on her face.

"This is super dumb," Tessa complained.

"They're not going to know the difference. They're morons," Kate said. "They spent an hour sniffing each other's butts!"

"I don't understand why I have to dress like the weirdo."

"This is how you get to be my friend again," Kate replied.

"I SAID I WAS SORRY!!!"

"And this is how you prove it," Kate said.

Finn and his friends watched them walk to the base of the tree with lazy curiosity, but they didn't budge.

"Okay, get down on your hands and knees like you're a cat," Kate said.

"You're nuts!"

"You're the one who said Stevie gets jealous of other cats. Just give it a chance!"

Tessa was reluctant, but she did as she was asked. Kate stood over her, patting her on the head.

"Nice kitty," Kate said loudly so her brother could hear.

"Easy! You're going to give me a concussion," Tessa said.

"Sorry."

"That's better. Just like that," Tessa explained. "Now scratch behind my ears."

"Like this? Does that feel good? What's that noise you're making?"

"I'm purring," Tessa said. "Cats purr when they're happy."

"You sound like a broken blender."

"Forget this! I feel like an idiot." Tessa was about to stand, but Kate stopped her.

"Wait! It's working."

Finn, Lincoln, and Tessa were slowly climbing down the tree and meowing complaints all the way.

"Keep petting me," Tessa said.

"Oh, you're such a sweet kitty," Kate said. "Yes, you are. You're a little precious treasure. Who loves you more than Mama? No one. That's right. No one loves you more than Mama."

Kate watched patiently until her brother and his friends hopped to the ground. They crawled on all fours around her, brushing up against her legs. Soon she was petting them as well.

"This is the weirdest day ever," Tessa said.

After a few good ear scratches, her brother, Lincoln, and Julep turned their attention to the milk.

"Okay," Kate whispered to Tessa as she crept over to get the fishing rod and the cucumber. "Get ready."

"I still don't get this part," Tessa said.

"It's a well-known fact that cats and cucumbers are bitter enemies," Kate said.

"Who told you that?"

"The internet, duh!" Kate insisted, and she slowly let the fishing line and the cucumber dip down between the three older kids. "Go over to the house and open the back door when they get close. Be ready. They're going to be completely freaked out!"

When Tessa got to the back door, Kate let the cucumber plop onto the ground in the center of the trio. Julep was the first to see it. She screeched and leaped straight up into the air. Finn and Lincoln did the same; then all three tore off running. The trash bags were stacked high, creating a path to the house. Her brother led the charge, his long white tail straight and agitated. He went up the back steps, but before Tessa could lock him and his feline friends in the house, he came to a screeching stop.

"Uh-oh," Tessa said.

"Uh-oh," Kate said.

All three of the cats made a mighty leap over the wall of unicorn trash bags, and raced toward the street. They were fast on their feet, and before long the girls lost all sight of them.

"That's not good!" Tessa said.

"No, it is not. They're going to infect the whole world," Kate replied. She imagined a planet where everyone was sick with space cooties, swatting at balls of yarn and scratching at furniture. She had to stop it.

"Now what?"

"Get your bike," Kate said. "Three cats are no match for the Cornies."

24

"Finn? Can you hear me?"

"Snap out of it, derp!"

"Should we try to carry him? We need to get out of this storm."

"I'm not carrying him. Maybe if we smack him. Can I smack him?" Lincoln asked.

Finn could hear his friends' voices. He could even feel the heavy rain coming down and soaking him, but none of it mattered. Zeke's revelation about his dad had rocked his world. His dad . . . a Time Ranger? Was that possible?

"Finn Foley, you have to listen to me," Julep said. "I know what Zeke said was a shocker, but—"

Finn shook off his trance and looked up at his bewildered friends.

"Everything I thought I knew about my dad is wrong! He didn't desert us. I kidnapped him and hid him away somewhere no one can find him. Now I hear he dressed like a cowboy and tracked down time-traveling criminals. I don't know what to believe anymore."

"We get it," Lincoln said. "It's just that we're standing in the middle of the street."

Finn's eyes finally focused on his new surroundings. Lincoln was right. They were standing in the center of South Street, the busiest road in Cold Spring. It was dark and cold, and the sewers were overflowing with rain. Rivers raced down both sides of the cobblestone street. He leaped over one and, along with his friends, huddled under the skinny awning of an antiques shop.

"So, this is 1987," he said.

"Any reason you picked this day?" Lincoln said.

"It's my mom's birthday," he explained. "It was the first date that popped into my head."

Finn studied both sides of the street. The storefronts were familiar, but the businesses were all wrong. The ice cream shop was now an insurance company. A sign over Finn's favorite pizza parlor now advertised something called JAZZERCISE. The fancy holistic pharmacy was a magazine store. There was an odd glass shack, no bigger than a closet, sitting on the corner nearest them. Finn peered at it and saw something inside that looked like a phone his grandpa used to own. Signs advertised bizarre products—a see-through version of Pepsi, a bunch of ugly toys called Cabbage Patch Kids, and a movie about a half man, half machine named RoboCop. Most of the parked cars on the street were big, long, and boxy. A woman with the biggest hair Finn had ever seen got out of one. Everything she wore was pastel, even her umbrella.

"Can we get out of this rain?" Lincoln asked. "I'm soaked to my undies."

"There!" Julep grabbed Finn's hand and pulled him down the street. Lincoln followed. Together, they stomped through puddles until finally pushing through the door of a store called Cold Spring Five-and-Dime.

They stood in the doorway, shivering and wiping the rain out of their eyes. The space was warm and bright, with rows and rows of shelves that went all the way to the back of the store. There were racks of men's pants, neckties, board games, school supplies, gardening tools, flip-flops, Halloween costumes, and Christmas ornaments. The place seemed to sell everything. A display advertised a sale on something called floppy disks, but Finn didn't have a clue what they were.

To the right was a long red counter with a row of stools and some matching tables scattered about. An apple pie rested under glass. Milkshake machines and a soda dispenser lined the wall, along with a big menu: burgers, fries, chili, fried fish sandwiches, soup. Reading it reminded Finn that he was hungry again.

A teenager with long hair tied back in a ponytail stood behind the counter watching them drip water on the floor. He gave Finn a hard look.

"Kid, Halloween isn't for three months," he said.

Finn glanced down at the cowboy pajamas. The entire left leg was blackened. Miller might have tried to kill them, but she was right. The time machine was officially busted.

"He lost a bet. He has to dress like that for a week," Lincoln lied.

"Bogus, dude." The teenager gestured to the stools by the counter. "Pop a squat."

"Huh?"

"Sit down."

The kids slid onto the stools as lightning lit up the front window. The storm was getting worse. Rain was coming down in sheets and the wind was blowing it sideways. A stop sign on the corner bounced around as if the weather were trying to yank it right out of the sidewalk.

"You want anything?" the teen asked, gesturing to the menu above him.

"Sorry, we don't have any money," Julep admitted.

"Figures. You know what? I'm feeling generous. Today's my last day and the boss left me in charge. How about three chocolate milkshakes, on the house?"

Finn watched him scoop vanilla ice cream into a silver cup, add milk and a squirt of chocolate syrup, followed by a heaping scoop of powdered malt. After a few whizzing moments on the mixer, he poured his creation into three tall glasses. They looked so good Finn almost cried.

Julep took a sip, leaving her with a chocolate mustache.

"OMG!" she whispered.

"I'm glad you like it."

"Thanks, so . . . wait a minute. Do I know you?" Lincoln asked. "No way! Mr. Doogan?"

Finn gawked at the teenager, fully aware his mouth was hanging wide open. If he used his imagination to get rid of the long hair and the pimples, then add about fifty pounds, there was no mistake. The kid behind the counter was their principal.

"Mr. Doogan? Dude, I'm not that much older than you," the teenager complained.

"Sorry, he calls everyone older than him 'Mister.' So, last day, huh?" Finn asked.

"Yep! I'm out of this town tomorrow morning. My band and I are moving down to the city to dedicate all our energy to our music," Doogan said. He reached over to a stack of flyers resting on the counter and handed one to Finn. A photograph of the band was in the center. There were five of them, dressed in tight, tiger-striped spandex pants. A few wore scarves wrapped around their necks and wristbands with metal studs. Under the picture were the words *Screaming Beauties,* which Finn guessed was the band's name. No one in the group was particularly beautiful, especially the bass player, who looked like he might be fifty years old. "Do you like heavy metal?"

"I don't know what that is," Lincoln said.

Doogan sighed.

"Everyone in this town is so behind the times," Doogan said. "Heavy metal is the music of the future. It's loud. It's in your face. Adults hate it. That's why it's so boss. You know, you should get my autograph now before I'm famous."

Doogan took a napkin out of the dispenser and signed his name. He handed it to Finn with a proud smile.

"Wow," Finn said as he pointed the date to his friends. "Thanks."

"Screaming Beauties, man! Remember that name. We're going to be huge. I'm so glad to be leaving this dump. Well, the boss will be back soon, and if the dishes aren't done he's going to have a cow. I hope I never see a sponge again!" he said before he disappeared into the kitchen.

"I guess Doogan's music career didn't work out,"

Lincoln said as he stared down at the flyer. "I have a feeling that's a good thing."

"This is where we're stuck? Forever?" Finn asked. He glanced over to Julep, hoping she might put a positive spin on the bad news, but she looked sad and distracted.

"Are you okay?"

Julep shrugged. He could tell she was trying to be strong, but he knew her well. Being stuck in the 1980s wasn't her biggest worry. She was doing her best to hide her heartbreak over Truman. Miller's shop promised a miracle for her brother. It wasn't fair how it all ended, and Finn felt responsible. The pajamas were busted. There would be no more time traveling, no more second chances, no more changing the past. They were stuck in 1987 now.

"So what's the plan?" Lincoln said as he finished his milkshake.

"The plan?" Finn asked.

"Yeah, how are we going to get back home?"

"Have you really not been paying attention?" Finn said. "We're not going anywhere."

"I've been paying attention! It's just not like the two of you to give up," Lincoln said.

"No one is giving up," Julep said. She took her pack off, set it on the counter, and rummaged through it until she found the What-U-Need. "We still have this. If we can

217

figure out how it works, maybe we can turn it into a new memory core. Maybe we could even turn it into medicine for my brother. I mean, anything's possible, right?"

"Um, I hate to bring this party down even more," Lincoln said. He pointed to the device. A jagged piece of metal was stuck in the side and it was leaking black ooze on the counter.

"What happened to it?" Finn asked.

Julep studied her pack, finding a tear in the side.

"A piece of shrapnel must have hit me during one of the explosions."

"One zipped past me, too. I'm super lucky, really. If it had hit my leg, I could have been really hurt," Lincoln said.

"Maybe if we pull it out?" Julep wondered. She grabbed the metal shard between her fingers and yanked, but it was stuck tight. Lincoln held on to the other side and pulled. Even working together, the shrapnel wouldn't budge.

"Here, let me try," Finn said to her, but Julep waved him off.

"I got it," she said. "It's starting to give. I can feel it."

Finally, with a groan, she fell backward onto the floor.

"Oww!"

"Are you okay?" Finn asked as he helped her stand.

"I cut myself." Julep showed him a nasty red slice across her palm. A mixture of blood and the strange oozing liquid of the What-U-Need was seeping into the wound. Finn snatched some napkins and pressed them against the cut to stop the bleeding while Lincoln called for Doogan to bring a first aid kit.

"What happened?" the teenager asked. He was wearing an apron and covered in suds.

"Just a dumb accident," she replied. "I need a bandage."

"You should wash the wound first," he said.

Julep agreed and hurried toward the ladies' room. Finn stood outside, pacing back and forth, worrying about his friend. The last thing the trio needed was another injury. Lincoln joined him, but instead of concern, he had a strange, silly look on his face. He was also hiding something behind his back.

"Lincoln, this isn't the time for goofing around," Finn snapped.

"I thought you'd want to see what I found in the kids' section," Lincoln said as he revealed a pair of pajamas on a hanger. They were decorated with little smiling cowboys riding little smiling ponies and they were the exact same size as the broken time-traveling pajamas he was wearing.

"No way!"

"Yes way!" Lincoln cried.

Julep stepped out of the bathroom and saw the pajamas, too.

"No way!" she shouted.

"That's what we said!" Finn cried.

"What are the odds that we'd find a pair just like the one you're wearing?" she asked.

"The other me was there during the snowstorm. He was obviously in the dome. I think it's totally possible he's been in this store. Maybe there are things Time wants to happen, no matter what we decide to do."

"Like it's a person?"

Finn shrugged.

"Zeke said he thought Time was alive and that it made choices," Finn said.

"Well, hey, Time! Send us home," Lincoln shouted into the air.

Julep held up the new pajamas to get a closer look.

"I wish I was smart enough to turn these into a time machine. That would solve a lot of our . . ." Julep's face went pale and she let out a little moan.

"Hey, this thing is glowing?" Doogan shouted from behind the counter. He pointed to the broken What-U-Need. The strange fluid pulsated red, then purple, then black again. All the while, Julep was trembling. She fell to the cold floor and groaned in pain. When Finn knelt beside her, he thought he saw her eyes turn completely black for a second.

"Hey, what's wrong with her?" Doogan said as he rushed over to help Julep onto her feet.

"An allergic reaction," Finn lied. He knew the What-U-Need was causing Julep's problems, but he didn't know how to explain it to Doogan.

"Let's get her into a chair," the teenager said, and with the help of the boys he sat Julep at one of the tables. Her shaking stopped, but now she was eerily quiet. While Finn and Lincoln exchanged worried expressions, Doogan doused the girl's wounded hand with antibacterial cream and wrapped it with gauze.

"We should call her parents," Doogan said.

"Her parents are still in diapers," Lincoln confessed.

"Huh?"

"She's fine. She just needs to rest," Finn said.

Suddenly, Julep's eyes popped open. The pinkness in her cheeks went back to normal. She smiled and looked as healthy as ever.

"Phew. You scared us pretty good," Finn said.

"You sit right here and rest. I've got to take out the trash before the boss comes back. After that, I'll drive you guys home," Doogan said. He went to the back, grabbed a couple of overstuffed garbage bags, and headed out the front door. The moment he was gone,

Julep leaped up and locked the door, then flipped the Open sign to Closed.

"We must act quickly. I need some things," she said. "Get me as much copper wiring as you can find, a pair of needle-nose pliers, a magnifying glass, anything made with steel, a couple of bags of sand—"

"Sand?" Finn said.

"Yes, for making silicone," she said.

"Uh, what's going on, Julep?" Lincoln said.

"I cannot explain it to you. It is far too complicated for your primitive minds—"

"Primitive minds?" Lincoln interrupted.

"I will make this as simple as possible. I am going to build a new time machine."

Both of the boys laughed until they saw that she was serious.

"Hurry!" she said. "I do not know how long I'm going to understand how to do it. Move! Now!"

The boys bolted around the store while Julep shouted for more things she needed. The five-and-dime sold a little of everything, from hardware, to clothes, to pots and pans.

"I need a grill!" she said. "Preferably one that uses charcoal."

"What for?" Finn asked.

"The fire," she replied.

Finn looked to Lincoln but it was clear he didn't know what was happening to their friend, either.

They found everything she asked for, including the grill, then rolled it all to the front in a wheelbarrow. She instructed Lincoln to fill the grill with charcoal briquettes and lighter fluid. Meanwhile, Finn stripped the plastic coating off a spool of wiring.

It wasn't long before Teenage Doogan returned. When he found the door locked, he knocked politely, but the high winds, terrible rain, and growing collection of store items the children were throwing into a pile next to a lit grill turned his knocks into angry pounding.

"Hey! Unlock the door! You have to pay for that!" he shouted.

"Ignore him! I need black electrical tape!" Julep cried.

"On it," Lincoln shouted as he ran down an aisle.

"Uh-oh," Finn said, pointing toward the door. "Mr. Doogan has a friend."

A short, bald, sour-faced man stood next to the teenager on the sidewalk outside. He held a cheap umbrella, but it was quickly taken by the wind. Soaked and cursing, he took a key chain out of his pocket. Julep darted to the door and twisted the knob just as he inserted a key, causing it to snap in half inside the lock. Both Doogan and the owner howled in anger.

"This is my shop, you juvenile delinquents!" He turned to Doogan and said something the kids couldn't hear. A moment later, the teen dashed away into the night.

The old man kept pounding on the door, but Julep ignored him completely. She was too busy with what looked like a mad science experiment. She cooked sand in a pot on the charcoal grill, used a microscope to thread tiny strands of copper into the pajama's fabric, and cut up stacks and stacks of floppy disks with a pair of scissors.

"Should we stop her?" Finn asked Lincoln.

"I don't have a clue, man," he said. "Honestly, I'm afraid of her."

"Can we get you anything?" Finn called out to her.

If she heard him, she ignored it. All of her attention was on her work.

Flashing red and blue lights now appeared outside the front window, along with several loud sirens.

"We are going to jail for maybe forever," Lincoln whispered.

"All right, kids," a voice boomed from outside. A white-haired sheriff appeared outside, wearing a raincoat and talking into a bullhorn. "Whatever prank you are pulling has got to stop right now. If you unlock the door and come out, we don't have to make this a big deal, but if you don't, things will get very,

very uncomfortable for you when we break the door down."

Finn turned to Julep to warn her, but she was busy pouring a thick brown liquid into a mold they found in the section that had ceramics supplies. The liquid had just been sand.

"They are almost done," she said as she grasped the mold with a pair of tongs and hurried behind the counter. She placed it into an ice cream tub, where a spray of hissing steam rose to the ceiling. "My apologies for their crude design. I am working with limited resources here in 1987, so the new pajamas are not as efficient as the first pair. The memory core had to be reimagined, and I am not particularly proud of the wiring, but it will work. Put them on over the old pair so its files can migrate to the new memory."

She tossed him the pajamas. When he caught them, he got a nasty zap to his fingers.

"Ow!"

"I had to re-create the internal battery. The old pair was fueled by cold fusion, a technology that does not exist in this time period. Inventing it wouldn't have been practical, so this new pair runs on static electricity," she explained. "Lincoln, we will need a bag of balloons."

Lincoln threw up his hands in surrender and hurried off to find some while Finn pulled the new pajamas on over the original set. As he was buttoning them up the front, Julep wiped the ice cream off the new memory core, then hurried over and attached it to the pajama's collar. Finn felt the familiar energy building inside them.

"All the core functions of the first pair are downloading into the second," Julep explained. "In essence, you never took the pajamas off, so time will not reset to the new normal."

"If you say so," Finn said. "I sort of wished we could have made the new time machine out of something else, something that fits," he said as he yanked and tugged at all the seams. The new pj's were no more comfortable than the first set.

"I've got the balloons," Lincoln said when he returned with a bag of them in his hand. Julep blew one up, tied it off, and then handed it back to Lincoln. "Give your friend a noogie."

Lincoln grinned, then rubbed the balloon against Finn's head. It was uncomfortable, but it worked. The energy in the pj's kept growing and growing.

"We're really going home?" Lincoln asked.

"Yes. We're going home," Finn said.

"Finn Foley, you are lying to us," Julep said.

"Huh?"

"Your breath quickened, and your eyes darted

toward the ceiling. You do that when you are not being honest," Julep explained.

Finn gawked at his friend. He should have been surprised that she could read him so well, but then again, she did just invent a time machine.

"What's going on, derp?"

"Fine. I'm taking you home but I'm going to try and finish what Old Man Finn asked me to do," he admitted. "I can't give up on my dad. I know it's probably impossible, but I still have to try."

"How? The Playlist was destroyed," Julep said.

"I think I found the final date in the library. There was a video of a battle we haven't seen. It's a long shot, I know. The old man said he had been fighting Paradox for sixty years, but it's all I've got to go on."

"You suck," Lincoln said.

"Huh?"

"You're going without us? We're your best friends."

"I know that but—"

"Do you think we would turn our backs on you when you need us?"

"I know you want to go home to see your mom and—"

"Really? It's one more date! You don't think I can do one more date? Are you dumb or am I wasting my time hanging around with you?"

"He is not very intelligent," Julep said.

The sheriff outside pounded on the glass window.

"We're going to break in. This is your last chance," he threatened.

Finn stared down at his feet, feeling ashamed and lucky at the same time. What had he done in his life to deserve friends like Lincoln and Julep?

A window shattered in the front of the store.

"Let's do this," Lincoln said, giving Finn's head a few more rubs with the balloon. "Where are we going?"

Finn held out his hand and the subatomic STICKY appeared, just the way the hologram librarian explained it would. A glowing screen floated above his palm with a date written on it.

March 3, 2069.

"Are you sure you're up for this?" he asked his friends.

Lincoln nodded.

"Let's do it," Julep said.

"All right, pajamas," he said. "Take us to March 3, 2069."

Finn's hair stood on end. He felt a charge in his fingertips, and a beautiful golden sphere appeared around them. He was never happier to see one. The sheriff and his deputies got the front door open and pushed into the store. They surrounded the kids, demanding they raise their hands over their heads.

"We are very sorry for the mess," Julep said, and in a flash of light, the Cold Spring Five-and-Dime, the entire sheriff's department of Cold Spring, and the keyboard player for the Screaming Beauties vanished in the blink of an eye.

25

Kate and Tessa pedaled their bikes as fast as they could. Finn, Lincoln, and Julep were way ahead, but they were also dumb and easily distracted. Shiny things and scurrying animals stole their attention. When they found them, Lincoln was swallowing a mouse he retrieved from a dumpster, and Finn and Julep were hiding under a parked car. The girls spooked them into someone's backyard, where they cowered under a picnic table. It was the least of their problems. Kate realized if they caught her brother and his friends, she and Tessa had no way to get them home. Desperate, she called her mom again, but there was still no answer.

"Seriously!" Kate said. "How long does she need to take a test?"

"Is there anyone else you can call?" Tessa asked.

"Not really," Kate said. Deputies Day and Dortch, who helped fight the Plague, went to work for the FBI in Washington, DC. Principal Doogan took a job in another town. All the people who would believe Finn was infected with a space virus were infected, too.

"Um, are you seeing this?" Tessa asked.

Finn, Lincoln, and Julep were glowing red, like there were stoplights inside them. Together, they howled like alley cats and looked up at the sky.

"What are they doing?" Tessa continued.

"I don't know, but it doesn't seem good," Kate replied. "Stevie doesn't glow, right?"

A whooshing sound stole their attention. When Kate turned, she saw a huge, shimmering circle directly behind her.

"What is that?" Tessa asked.

"Hide! Something weird usually comes out of these things," Kate warned, and together she and Tessa scurried behind a toolshed.

Kate was right about weird. As they watched from behind the shed, they saw a woman with dark brown skin and silver hair step through the portal. She was wearing a cowboy costume and carrying two golden guns. Behind her came a walking egg as tall as Finn, also wearing the Western clothes. In fact, everyone who walked through the portal, from the man with a groundhog's head to a giant wolf to a boxy robot, was dressed like they were going trick-or-treating. Behind them was the biggest man Kate had ever seen. He was dressed from head to toe in black except for a white bandanna that hid his face. Next to him was a snarling, monstrous dog, followed by an enormous carrot wearing a dress.

"Tracker, you have my apologies," the woman said. Her revolvers were burning white-hot, just like her hair. "We made duplicates of the criminals. Their crisis alarms have gone off. It can only mean one of two things: someone has figured out that they're imposters, or the clones are having troubles they can't get out of on their own. It's unfortunate for us, but the truth is they serve an important purpose. We'll scoop them up and take them back to the Barn for repairs, then find Finn and his friends."

"I tried to tell you these clones weren't ready," the carrot lady said.

Kate watched in stunned silence as the man with a groundhog head tried to corral her brother and his friends. The trio ran off, hissing and shrieking, forcing the strange alien to chase after them.

"Clones?" Kate whispered.

"Miss Ellie, there's something that needs to be said," the carrot continued. "Zeke and I go way back, and well, the gossip about him don't make any sense. Zeke ain't the kind to turn his back on his own, unless there's a real powerful reason. He's done a lot of good since he joined this team, and I say he deserves a chance to explain himself."

"Cookie, I appreciate your loyalty," Miss Ellie said. "But Zeke has been trouble since Asher recruited him, and now he's gone and shown his true colors to us all. Asher stuffed his brain with a lot of cockamamie ideas, too, but at least he did his job and stayed out of trouble. It's a shame what happened to him, and I understand Zeke feels he owes the man, but the universe is more important than a kid, no matter who his father happens to be."

"They're talking about my dad," Kate whispered.

"Those freaks know your dad?" Tessa asked.

"Well, I'll leave you to it. I better help capture the copycats." The carrot frowned, then hurried in the direction of her clones.

"We need to get back on their trail," the giant man said. "The dog smells them, though it seems confused."

"This is where they live," the wolf said. It scanned the neighborhood, forcing Kate and Tessa to duck out of sight. "I came here with Asher once."

"We need to get out of here, now!" Kate said, gesturing to her friend to follow. They'd barely made a move when one of the cowboy creatures, the huge violet blob with big eyes, turned the corner and slithered into their path. The girls were so surprised they were knocked off their feet.

"Miss Ellie! Take a look at this," it gurgled.

"What is it, Enos?" the woman said as she approached. "Well, well, well. What have we got here?"

"Dagnabbit!" the robot said. "Pearl, you were supposed to drop us into a place where no one would see us."

"I did the best I could!" the egg cried.

"Stop your fussing," the wolf said. Its angry eyes felt like they were burning Kate's skin. "This is a good thing. These two aren't a couple of nobodies. This one is Finn Foley's sister, Kate."

The robot and a being that looked like a walking asparagus clamped their hands down on the girls and dragged them to their feet.

"Get your hands off us," Kate shouted. She and Tessa tried to squirm free, but they weren't strong enough.

"Your brother has been a burr in my britches for far too long," Miss Ellie said.

Just then, the carrot lady and the groundhog man returned with Finn, Lincoln, and Julep attached to leashes.

"We got 'em," she said. "Wasn't easy, either. I'm covered with scratches."

"Good. Take them back to the Ranch," Miss Ellie said. "Tex, open a portal for her."

Kate watched the groundhog man remove a lasso hanging from his waist. When he spun it, a flaming portal just like the one that had brought them appeared. She watched the carrot lead her brother and his friends toward it. They fought and struggled against her every step of the way. Desperate, Kate broke free of the asparagus man and jumped in front of the glowing doorway to block the carrot's path.

"If that's not my brother," Kate shouted, "where is he? Where is the real Finn Foley?"

Tessa yanked herself free as well and rushed to stand by Kate.

"This is probably the limit of me trying to earn your forgiveness," she mumbled.

"Understood," Kate replied.

"Get those two out of the way," Miss Ellie commanded.

"Just try to get past us," Kate said.

The man in black snatched the girls by the backs of their shirts and lifted them off the ground. With the path clear, Cookie led Finn, Lincoln, and Julep into the portal and they disappeared.

"You won't get away with this," Kate promised.

"Miss Ellie, these two have seen a lot. Considering one of them is a Foley, I advise we take them back to the Ranch, too. Cookie can erase their memories," the robot said.

"No," the man in black grunted.

"You have a better idea, Tracker?" Miss Ellie asked.

"We've wasted enough time and energy chasing the criminals when there is a much easier way to capture them. We're going to wait for them to come to us."

26

Zeke considered himself lucky when he got back to the Ranch. The other Rangers were nowhere in sight. They were either searching the continuum for him or, worse, hunting Finn, Julep, and Lincoln. He hoped Asher's son was smart enough to keep moving until he could find them himself. Confronting his teammates was something he could no longer avoid, but first he had to prepare for the fight of his life. It was up to him to stop Paradox.

Luckily, the Ranch housed the universe's greatest collection of weapons, seized from time criminals locked in the Barn. He gathered the most explosive and dangerous, then packed them in a sack. He couldn't help but feel like a hypocrite. Owning one of these weapons was enough to get you imprisoned, and now here he was stealing a dozen of them. Old Man Finn would laugh in his face, but these were desperate times. In his collection was a Mini Black Hole Emitter from the twenty-third century, a hypersonic whistle from 2318, three different shoulder-mounted atomic missile launchers from 2424, and a laser crossbow he'd swiped out of the hands of a sleeping seven-foot-tall dogman in the year 2801. He also had a handful of chrono grenades and a cold-fusion sword. Would it be enough to stop Paradox? He couldn't be sure, but he had to try. Now all he needed was a team.

In the past, he would have turned to the Rangers for help, but they had never had much interest in going after Paradox. He doubted he'd get much help now that he was a traitor. It was time to get creative.

The Ranch was crowded with workers, still busy repairing the damage from the time twisters. With his sack of weapons strapped to his back, he crept from cactus to cactus until he reached the base of the windmill. Built on a wooden scaffold, its blades spun forty feet off the ground, generating electric power for the ranch house and the Barn. Once there, he scanned the area to make sure no one was watching, then reached into his bag of goodies for a stick of dynamite. He lit the fuse, watched it spark, and leaned it against one of the windmill's four posts. Then he ran.

The explosion nearly knocked him over. Horses and cows cried out in fear. The windmill's scaffolding crumbled and caused the whole structure to tip. It fell on the fence that held the piglets, setting the tiny oinkers free.

When the workers came to investigate, Zeke circled around to the other side and dashed into the Barn. Inside, he scurried up a ladder to the second floor, where the prisoners' cells began. There he found the control panel for the force fields that trapped the inmates. There were so many buttons, thousands of them, but Zeke knew exactly which five he needed to push. He released them one by one. A loud alarm rang, and then a heavy clang as the energy prisons that kept the bad guys locked up deactivated. Five criminals wandered forward, confused, angry, and eager for revenge. Zeke wasn't sure he was making the right decision, but it was the best of a bunch of terrible ideas.

"We need to talk," he said when they were standing face to face with him. These were the worst criminals in the Barn. Ranks Forgolian held an entire planet hostage when he threatened to change its history, Narlian Crager caused a galaxy to collapse as revenge on a bully who picked on him in school, Dunka Maxx stole an entire century and sold it on the black market, Pert 77 left his time portal open so long it sucked in a neighboring planet, and Cheet Bering was an assassin for hire who murdered the ancestors of enemies. Each of them eyed Zeke with a mixture of rage and murder. "I have an offer to make you."

"Is this some kind of joke, Ranger?" Cheet Bering asked.

"Do I look like I'm laughing? I'm going to let you out. All you have to do is what you do best—cause mayhem."

"We're listening," Pert 77 said.

"I'm forming a posse. I have a problem the Rangers refuse to address, so we're going to take care of it ourselves."

"What's this problem called?" Dunka Maxx asked.

"Paradox," Zeke said.

The prisoners grumbled. A few of them looked fearful. It seemed rumors about the monster had spread throughout the entire Barn.

"That's suicide," Narlian said.

"You five are the meanest, orneriest, no good, backstabbing lowlifes in all of history. I never would have believed you were yellow. All right, fine. I'll put you back in your cells."

"We didn't say no. We said it was suicide," Dunka said as she looked back at the other criminals. "What do we get if we take care of your problem?"

"I'll personally escort you back to your home worlds, or at least one that's close by that still exists," Zeke promised. "I can't guarantee the Time Rangers won't come looking for you, but if you find something to do that doesn't involve messing with the timeline, I suspect you'll be overlooked."

"Do we get to keep the weapons?" Ranks asked.

Zeke nodded. All five of the criminals smiled.

"We got a deal, Ranger," Dunka said.

"Deal," Cheet said.

"Nice to hear," Zeke said. "Who wants the laser crossbow?"

21

March 3, 2069. There was no way to know if this was where they would find Old Man Finn, but it was a battle zone. They could hear it all the way down the street.

"You stay here," Finn told Julep. She looked sweaty and weak, and with each passing minute she seemed to get worse. The cut on her hand was causing it to swell. He was worried she might die.

"No," she replied. Her voice was weak, not much more than a whisper. "I'm going with you. I can see things. It's hard to explain, but it's like I can sense possibilities. I've done the math in my head, and if you don't take me, you have a very small chance of surviving. I am a lot smarter than I was this morning and I could be a big help. I just need a second to catch my breath."

"Not a chance, Julep Li," Finn said.

"He's right," Lincoln said to her.

"Fine! Leave me here to miss it all. But at least take some pictures. This is a big moment."

She reached into her pack and pulled out her phone. The trio huddled together and Finn took a picture.

Might be the last picture we take together, he thought.

Without warning, Julep collapsed in the street. The boys helped her to a bench outside an abandoned store. Finn called her name, but she didn't respond.

"She needs a doctor," Lincoln said. "This isn't the flu."

"I don't think it's going to matter," Finn said.

"Huh?"

"Lincoln, when this is over, and I take the pajamas off, there's a very good chance the whole world is going to be different. We made changes on these trips, and you and I . . . we might not be friends anymore."

"I know."

"If that's true, then there's a good chance that I'm not going to be friends with Julep, either," Finn explained.

"Why? You will still be at the same school. Why wouldn't you be friends?"

"'Cause I . . . Before you, I couldn't talk to her. I felt like barfing every time she came around. She made me too nervous."

"Yeah, you have a crush on her!" Lincoln said.

Finn felt his cheeks turn pink.

"Well, maybe this is for the best. If you don't meet me and you're too chicken to talk to her, then none of this happened and she isn't going to get sick."

Finn nodded, following his friend's logic. It was a silver lining in a very dark cloud.

"Let's go do this. She'll be safe here and when we're done, we'll come back and get her," Finn said. He slid her cell phone into his pants and together the boys laid their friend down on the bench. When she was as comfortable as they could make her, they turned their attention to the fight and started walking in its direction.

"Sounds like Paradox is pretty angry," Lincoln said.

"Seems like every version of us has a way of getting under its skin."

They heard shouting.

"C'mon," Finn said, and they took off at a sprint. Farther up the street they saw Paradox, hovering in a ball of fire. Two men were running in its direction. One was Old Man Finn, the other Old Man Lincoln. They confronted the monster. Whatever they said caused the fireball to vanish, and Paradox landed on its feet.

"Over here!" Lincoln said, and the kids found shelter behind a tree. They peered around it, watching from afar.

"What are they doing?" Finn asked.

"Hard to tell," Lincoln replied. "I have to say, time

travel isn't a lot of fun, but at least I got a super-cool robot leg out of it."

The boys watched Old Man Finn point a strange device at Paradox. When he unleashed it, the monster screamed in agony. The energy coming out of the weapon looked like it was ripping the skin right off the monster. Paradox fought but kept getting pushed back by the blasts. Old Man Finn was relentless. He kept hammering the creature, but then, for some reason, the machine petered out. He shook it, trying to get it to start up again, but when it didn't, he threw it to the ground.

Paradox recovered quickly. He snatched Old Man Finn by the wrist. When his partner charged forward, the monster wrapped its hand around his neck, then zapped him in the head with a bolt of lightning. The attack sent Old Man Lincoln tumbling to the ground. He didn't get up.

Lincoln gasped.

"Noooooo!" Old Man Finn shouted.

"It just killed me," Lincoln said as he lifted his Chrono-Disrupter.

"You want to suck it into that?" Finn said. "We tried that already."

"We're going to try it again."

As the kids slinked along the road, Old Man Finn

fell to his hands and knees. Paradox stood over him. It looked as if it was going to kill him, but a golden sphere encircled the old man. Paradox raged. It pounded on the bubble with angry fists, but it was strong. Nothing Paradox did stopped it and a second later, Old Man Finn and his time machine were gone, leaving the two boys alone with a monster.

It looked up and saw them, then laughed out loud.

"Have you come to kill me, too?"

"We came to try," Finn said.

Paradox dashed toward them in a flash. Its horrible, empty face was suddenly mere inches from Finn's own.

"Tell me, Finn Foley," Paradox said. "Where is your father?"

"Why are you asking me?" Finn said, doing his best not to sound frightened. "Nobody tells me anything around here. Why do you want to know?"

"Asher Foley tried to kill me the day I was born," Paradox said, his voice dripping with bitterness. "I escaped but never truly recovered. I am a broken thing, and for a time I believed my destiny was robbed from me. But now I see what I was meant to do. It's obvious! I am here to rewrite this world, to tear it apart and recreate it fresh and new. I will take on the role of Time itself! But your father must be there to watch me rise to glory. I want him to see that his efforts were for nothing. I suppose I have something to show you as well, Finn, I know you have wondered what is beneath this black shell. Would you like to take a peek?

"I promise what you see will change your life." Paradox laughed. "Maybe I'm your father. Oh! Wouldn't that be a delicious twist? Gasp. Maybe it's you! Or an evil twin? Or your sister?"

"Stop playing games with me!" Finn demanded.

"Oh, you're no fun. And to think you've had the answer all along." Paradox giggled.

"How's that?" Lincoln said.

"Check Julep's phone. I bet she's got a picture of me. Go on, take a peek."

Finn tentatively removed Julep's phone from his pocket. He opened up the photo app and scanned through thousands of shots. There were images of the strange time tubes, and the mastodon, and the futuristic freeway jammed with traffic, but he saw pictures he didn't recognize, too, spanning many years in the lives of the other Finn, Lincoln, and Julep. This must have been the data Miller moved from the other Julep's phone. In each one the trio got a little older. Finn spotted one where Julep and he were trying to take a picture together. They must have been ten years older. She was kissing him on the cheek. The other Finn seemed both surprised and happy.

And then he found a video. The older Julep was sitting in an empty room, wrapped in blankets. Her eyes were sunken and she looked feverish. Every few moments her body shook with chills.

"I made a mistake. I shouldn't have been messing with what we stole from the dome. The What-U-Need broke in my hand and . . . Finn and Lincoln don't know how bad it is. I can't tell them, especially Finn. It will break his heart now that we finally got the courage to be honest with one another. I . . ." Julep started coughing. It got worse and worse, and then she spit something black into her hand.

"What is that?" Lincoln asked.

More of it crept out of her mouth—a drop at first, but then it poured out like a faucet. It swam down her neck and around the back of her head, until it completely covered her face. The phone fell from her hand and bounced around on the floor. Finn could hardly breathe. He knew what was about to happen. Paradox leaned into the camera. It laughed, as if it knew Finn was watching, and then the screen went black.

"No," Finn said.

"That can't be true!" Lincoln shouted.

"Surprise!" Paradox giggled.

"You can't be Julep," Finn shouted.

"Oh, I'm afraid it's true. And before you give me some courageous speech about how you're going to save her, let me be very clear: She's not here. She's not hiding under any layers, waiting for someone to free her. She's gone. There is only me now."

Lincoln roared. He raised the Chrono-Disrupter and fired it at the monster. The energy blast hit Paradox, but like before, it had no effect. He tried again and again, but nothing hurt it.

"Oh, Lincoln," Paradox said as the tips of its fingers sparked. "This is going to be fun. I've never killed the same person twice in one day."

There was a blast, but not at Lincoln. Something hit Paradox in the back, and it fell forward onto its knees. When the smoke cleared, Finn saw six figures standing behind the fallen monster. They were aliens, some covered in scars. One had a metal hand. Another a patch over his eye. They were all carrying bizarre weapons, and leading them was a copper-skinned cowboy with metal implants on either side of his head.

"Zeke!" Finn cried.

"Sit tight, boys," Zeke said. "We'll take it from here."

The crowd unleashed all their weaponry at once, pulverizing the black nightmare. The monster was completely overwhelmed. It struggled to stand, but the assault was too much.

Paradox was on one knee and glowing like the sun. It roared with rage. When it clapped its hands together, it sounded as if the Earth had split open, and a wave of heat and power sent them tumbling. In the fall, Lincoln dropped his Chrono-Disrupter. It bounced and landed at Finn's feet.

"Boys," Zeke said. "It's too strong! Run!"

"Not yet," Finn said. He got to his feet, snatched the Chrono-Disrupter off the ground, and aimed it at Paradox.

"We already tried to suck it in," Lincoln said.

"I know. How do you let everything out?" he asked Zeke.

"Push the button three times."

Finn did what he was told. One. Two. Three.

The first thing that hit Paradox was the mastodon. It appeared in the air and sailed down the street, slamming into the monster. Then came the saber-tooths. They circled Paradox and sprang on it, slashing with their claws and tusks. Paradox wailed, doing its best to fight them off. Next came the tree. It flew down the road and hit the monster, sending it sailing back several yards.

Much to Finn's surprise, Paradox managed to stand. It lumbered forward, limping and dazed.

"Hey! That's mine," Lincoln said, and he snatched the weapon from Finn's hands. He aimed it, pressed the button, and fired a cannonball into Paradox's gut. Four thousand soldiers followed and charged at the creature. Together, they unloaded their weapons and stabbed at it with pitchforks and shovels. The assault forced the monster back to the ground.

Paradox lay there and laughed.

"You think this can stop me? You will never stop me!"

A white Jeep landed on top of it, followed by one of the largest statues Finn had ever seen. It arced into the sky above them and came down on top of Paradox. The walking horror screamed just as the Heroes of Cold Spring crushed it flat.

For the first time since their arrival, the street was quiet.

Zeke took the Chrono-Disrupter from Lincoln.

"Is it dead?" Finn asked.

"If it's dumb enough to crawl out from under there, it will still have to deal with us," Zeke said. "Boys, where's Julep?"

"We left her on a bench down the street," Finn explained. "She's sick. She's going to turn into Paradox!"

"We need to get her to the Barn. The universe will be safe if we can get her into a cell, but it has to happen now. If you wait much longer all of this will happen again."

Finn and Lincoln raced down the street. They found Julep where they left her. She was shivering and coughing worse than before. Together, they helped her to her feet.

"Are we really taking her to the Barn?" Lincoln asked.

"If we take her there, she turns into Paradox. The only chance of saving her is to take her home. We can stop all of this if I just take off the pajamas."

28

The golden bubble materialized in Finn's backyard. It popped, and the smell of warm summer air filled his nose. He looked around to make sure they were in the right place. His mom's hammock was nearby, full of notebooks and highlighters. The house was intact. Everything seemed right except for the pathway made of trash bags that led from the big pine tree to the back door.

"So this is it?" Lincoln said, easing Julep into the soft grass. "I thought we'd have time to . . . you know, to say goodbye."

"We still have a chance," Finn said. "All we have to do it take off the pajamas."

"I don't understand, derp," Lincoln said.

"We changed things in the past, things that will affect us once I take them off."

"You mean my mom?" Lincoln said.

Finn nodded. "If your mom was around your whole life, chances are you didn't get kicked out of every school in town, which means we never met, never got into trouble, never became friends, and never went through time together. If that is the new normal, then I probably never met Julep. None of this will happen. Not to me, not to Old Man Finn, not any of us. It all gets erased."

It was a cruel way to end things, but there was no choice, and Lincoln knew it.

"You're going to be fine," Lincoln promised. "I'm kind of a pain in the butt, if you haven't noticed. You're better off without me."

"Don't do that," he said. "Don't act like it doesn't matter."

"Okay. I won't. It matters." Lincoln extended his hand and Finn shook it.

"Who knows what could happen? Maybe you'll take the pajamas off and I'll still be here. So let's not say goodbye."

"Then what do we say?" Finn said.

"See you around, derp."

"Not if I see you first," Finn replied.

Julep let out a painful moan. It was time. He couldn't

let his friend suffer another second. He unfastened the buttons, but an angry voice stopped him.

"Don't move a muscle."

Finn was stunned to see Miss Ellie come out the back door of his house, her revolvers in hand. Ten other Rangers followed, as well as the Tracker. The enormous brute had one hand clamped on his sister Kate's arm, and the other held on to her friend Tessa. A hulking dog lumbered out, snarling with rage.

"Not these losers again," Lincoln grumbled.

"You don't understand what's happening," Finn explained. "My friend is sick. She's going to turn into another Paradox if I don't take these off."

"Don't tell me what I understand, boy," Miss Ellie roared. "Now put your hands up real high and keep your mouth shut."

Julep staggered to her feet.

"I'm sorry, Finn. I can't fight it anymore," she said as a stream of black gunk leaked out of her mouth and down her shirt. Finn watched it creep around her torso, down her legs, and along her arms. He shouted for her to be strong, but it was too much for her. A moment later, she was covered from head to toe. Julep was gone. Now there was only Paradox.

"Now, where were we?" it asked.

"You remember us?" Lincoln said slowly.

"Foolish boy. I am not chained to Time!" Paradox

said. "In fact, I have never been more powerful. All of the weaknesses I had before are gone. Finn's father was not around to hurt me this time. I'm born again!"

Paradox waved its hand and a white light swept across the lawn. Lincoln dove to avoid it. Finn knocked his sister and Tessa to the ground, but everyone else wasn't so quick. It enveloped the Rangers, the Tracker, and his Hound. Their bodies twisted, like they were wet towels someone was trying to ring out. They cried in horror, as they got tighter and tighter, until they were nothing at all. Even the ugly dog vanished.

"Time, can you hear me?" Paradox shouted. "You're no longer needed. I've come to take over. You did your best, but let's be honest. I can do better!"

The monster raised its hands above its head. High in the sky, the clouds above Cold Spring formed a swirling black hurricane. Lightning shot out of the center and streaked downward, blasting trees and houses.

"I can do anything," it continued. "Time bends to my will!"

From behind the house stepped a snarling T. rex. It raced toward the children but was stopped when an army of futuristic soldiers appeared out of thin air and fired their laser rifles at it. Cavemen charged through the streets chasing a man driving a Model T. Silver flying saucers dipped out of the clouds and pirates raced through the backyards with sabers in their hands. Everywhere Finn looked there were people and creatures plucked from different time periods causing chaos in his neighborhood, and Paradox was the source. It didn't need a lasso or a pair of high-tech pajamas. It had a stranglehold on Time itself.

"Finn! What's happening?" Kate cried.

"It's the end of the world, little unicorn," Paradox said.

Finn looked down at the pajamas; then he looked at Lincoln.

Paradox laughed. "Boy, you are as predictable as your father. Do you think you can just erase me?"

"Gimme a balloon," he whispered to his friend.

Lincoln reached into his pocket and handed him one.

"What are you going to do, Foley?"

"I'm going to ruin a birthday party," Finn said after he blew it up and tied it into a knot. He rubbed the balloon on his head and could feel the static power growing stronger and stronger. "Pajamas, take me to August 16, 1987!"

The golden bubble swallowed him, and he was gone.

29

The wind and rain surprised him. The storm had slipped his mind. Too many things had happened the night of August 16, 1987, for him to remember some bad weather. Unfortunately, he'd also forgotten something important. The time machine didn't move him to different locations. The Cold Spring Five-and-Dime was downtown, a mile away. He had no choice but to run.

Once there, he saw the golden bubble appear out of thin air. It popped almost immediately, revealing Lincoln, Julep, and himself inside. If he didn't move quickly, he wouldn't beat them into the store.

Ducking behind a car, he crept along the sidewalk, careful to stay out of sight. If the other Finn saw him, they would splinter the timeline again, and he'd have a whole set of new problems on his hands.

"What in the world are you doing?" a woman said as he slunk by her car. He had seen her before, the first time he'd visited 1987. She was dressed from head to toe in pastels.

"Sorry," he said, then darted through the puddles, across the street, and through the front door of the store. He scampered down an aisle without stopping, hoping Doogan wouldn't see him, then found a closet and hid inside.

A moment later, he heard the bell on the door jingle. Cracking the closet door an inch, he watched Finn, Julep, and Lincoln enter. They were soaked and miserable. Doogan invited them to sit down. Then, just like before, he made them some chocolate milkshakes. It made Finn queasy to see it all play out again.

It was then that Julep took the What-U-Need out of her pack and set it on the counter.

With very little light, Finn searched the closet for anything that might cause a diversion. There, on the wall, was the fuse box. He was very familiar with the one at his house—lights were always going on and off in the old dump. He had to go down into the basement at least once a week to pop the circuit breakers, especially if someone used the microwave and the hair dryer at the same time. Inside the box were switches that turned the power off to every light and appliance in the store.

He flipped every single one to the off position. The five-and-dime plummeted into darkness. He heard himself cry out.

"What's going on?" Lincoln shouted.

"Stay right there," Doogan said. "It's the circuit breaker."

Finn slinked out of the closet and into the shop just before Doogan entered. This was his chance. With all his speed, he raced to the front of the store, snatched the What-U-Need, and spun toward the front door. Unfortunately, he tripped over his own feet and fell to the floor.

"Someone's in here!" Julep shouted.

A body fell on top of him. He assumed it was Lincoln. He was heavy and strong.

"What do you think you're doing?" he asked.

Finn squirmed away but the boy held on tight. Desperate, he kicked his best friend in the belly. All the air shot out of Lincoln's lungs, and he was free. With the What-U-Need in hand, Finn scampered to his feet, pushed open the front door, and darted into the storm just as a ball of flame appeared in the middle of the street. Cars were engulfed, a box full of newspapers was flung down the street, and the stop sign bent over permanently. Paradox had arrived. Finn looked up. In the lightning and streetlamps its face looked like it was melting.

"Like father, like son. Oh, you're a clever one, aren't you, Finn Foley," it said. "If Julep doesn't cut herself with the What-U-Need, I never exist. Was that your plan? I'll admit, it's much kinder than what your father tried to do to me."

A ball of electric energy sailed at Finn. He ducked down and it smashed into the window of the shop, breaking it and setting the front of the store on fire. He didn't waste a second. Finn bolted down the street with Paradox hovering in his ball of fire overhead.

"What will you do now, little boy? Have you any more ideas? Are we going to do the hide-and-seek game again for the next sixty years? I promise you, hiding from me will not be as easy this time. I am everywhere and in everything now."

Paradox was toying with him. The monster could kill him at any second and was only allowing this to happen because of some sick joy it got out of torturing him. Finn wanted to scream in anger. No matter what he did, Paradox won. It might always be like this. Would he be on the run like Old Man Finn, doomed to fight and fail forever? Was this how Time wanted it? Zeke thought it was alive, that it made choices, and picked winners and losers. It couldn't possibly want this to be how everything ended. Could it?

Maybe, but he had to take the chance. The answer to ending this nightmare suddenly came to him. It was horrible, but it might save everyone, and what other choice did he have? So with all his strength, he pulled on the shrapnel still lodged inside the What-U-Need. If he pulled it out himself, Julep could never cut her hand on it and transform into Paradox. She would never become the monster. In fact, Paradox would never exist. With one fateful jerk, the metal came free, but oh no! He sliced the palm of his hand. His blood mixed with the black chemicals inside the device, invading the wound and burning a path through his veins.

"I wish I could save everyone," he said, making a wish much like the one Julep made before she invented the time machine. The answer came as a sudden burst of energy. He could feel all his senses working overtime. He was suddenly smarter. He knew his plan would work. He knew he was the only one who could stop Paradox.

"Pajamas, take me home," he shouted.

30

The golden sphere appeared in his backyard just moments after he left. His sister, Tessa, and Lincoln were waiting, huddled together. Kate was crying and when she saw her brother's face, she ran and wrapped her arms around him.

"Is it over?" Lincoln asked.

"Not yet," he said just as the monster's fireball appeared. Paradox was chasing him across time, just as he hoped.

"This is getting boring," it said.

"I promise things are going to get very interesting in just a second. One more thing: if she's in there, if a hint of Julep Li exists in your heart, tell her she's one of the best friends I ever had," he said, then turned to Lincoln. "And you're the other, derp."

Without another word, he unbuttoned his pajamas and squeezed out of them, as well as the broken pair that were underneath. Soon they were in a pile on the ground.

"I'm still here," Lincoln said. "See! We were worried for—"

A sound like rushing water drowned out the boy's voice. Finn watched as Lincoln's clothes changed from a green T-shirt and jeans to a prep school uniform with a golden eagle crest on the lapel.

Lincoln looked down at himself, then gave Finn a sad smile.

"You're not so bad, Finn Foley," he said, and then he faded away.

Tessa was the next to vanish, then Kate. She re-appeared in her bedroom window, safe and sound. Paradox, however, was fighting the changes. It squirmed and its body bloated and shriveled, like the breath coming in and out of a balloon. The black shell that served as its skin cracked. Julep stepped out of it and then she vanished as well. Paradox, however, remained.

"That must be so disappointing," Paradox said when they were alone. "All those changes to Time and I am still here. I will tell you the same thing I told the old version of you, Finn Foley. Fighting me is pointless. I am Time itself, or rather, I soon will be."

Finn summoned all his courage and stepped close to the monster.

"No, you won't be. You see, I can beat you because I know something you don't. I'm you." He grabbed Paradox by the hands and held them tight. The monster pulled away, suddenly understanding what Finn was doing. With the poison inside his blood, Finn was on his way to becoming the new Paradox, and now he was committing the biggest no-no of time travel. Rule number three—never make direct contact with yourself.

"You realize what you've done, right? The universe will unravel," Paradox cried out. There was terror in his voice.

"It's a strong possibility, but you would erase everything and everyone I love anyway. I might be breaking everything before you have a chance to do it yourself, but I heard this theory: Time is alive. It chooses what happens to us. It picks winners and losers. If it is true, my only chance to stop you is to force Time to make a choice. All or nothing. You or me!"

Everything started to shake around them as if they were caught in an earthquake. Windows shattered. Car alarms blared. The tree in the backyard fell over with a *crack!* Everything twisted, then unwound, and then unraveled into ribbons that fluttered into the wind. Finn watched his own body drift away into the storm. Paradox unraveled as well.

"Noooooo!" it roared as its face unspooled like a roll of paper towels.

31

And then there was nothing, just endless white oblivion.

Finn was solid and alive, or at least it seemed that way to him. He looked around at his surroundings, unsure if he was inside something like a box, or outside something. He couldn't tell. All he knew for sure was that he was alone.

"Hello?"

His voice echoed into the nothing. It made him angry. Had he destroyed the universe? Had he gambled and lost? And if so, why was he still alive? Well, maybe Time wasn't alive, but if it was, he was going to unload some frustrations.

"So that's it, huh? I broke everything and you're just going to let it happen?" he cried. "I gave you a choice—

the monster who wanted to destroy you and take over your job, or the kid from Cold Spring who stopped it—and you picked neither? That sucks, dude. Am I wrong about you? Are you just a cold machine? Mindless? Brainless? Dumb, and with no heart? Wow! Did I blow it or what?"

He waited, hoping someone or something might step out of the whiteness and sit down for a chat. Maybe he'd get an explanation about how the universe worked, or a thank-you, but there was no big reveal. No one came out from behind the curtain.

"But if that's true, why am I still here?" he asked. He pinched himself just to be sure and felt the pain. He was breathing, so he wasn't dead.

But still there was nothing, and his fear and frustration took over. He stomped around. The whiteness didn't seem to have a border. He ran in one direction for a while, but nothing changed.

"You let me destroy the universe! Do you know how much that sucks! And you're keeping me alive. Why? Are you lonely? Are you torturing me? Is that what this is about? Well, it's not cool. I have family and friends. My dad is still out there. My mom and my sister need me. You can't just not choose! You have to make a choice!

"There's so much good stuff in the world worth saving—pizza with pineapple and ham, and dogs, and video games, and my mom, and my sister most of the time. And Lincoln. And Julep! You're going to throw all that away?"

Finn sat down. He felt stupid. This was silly. He was talking to himself. There was no one listening.

"Well, fine," he whispered.

He sat there for a long time, or maybe it wasn't so long. It was hard to tell. He was ready to get up and stretch his legs when he felt something tickling his foot. He looked down and watched a green bud break through the nothing.

"What's this?" he cried out.

The bud became a sapling and then a tree, growing taller and wider, so that it pushed him aside. It grew and grew, creaking and stretching until it was an enormous pine tree. In fact, it was the same pine tree in his backyard. He saw the roof of his house push itself up out of the white and rise higher and higher like it was a living thing, too. To his left and right he saw a line of houses doing the same, along with fences and swing sets and garages and cars, all popping up like flowers in the spring. The ground beneath him sprouted with bright green grass that grew and spread in every direction like it was paint on an artist's brush. The whiteness above him became a night sky. Clouds drifted across it and a bright yellow moon streaked in an arch across a star-filled universe. Crickets chirped. Soon the white was gone and the world was back.

Inside his house he saw his mom cooking in the kitchen window. He heard his sister singing in an upstairs bedroom.

"Thank you," Finn said aloud. "Good choice."

A shimmering portal of light appeared and from it stepped Zeke with his fiery lasso.

"You survived," Finn said.

"It's a bad habit of mine," the Ranger replied. "Unfortunately, my colleagues weren't so lucky."

"Yes, I saw. I'm sorry. So it's just you on the Ranch?"

"Well, the ranch hands and workers are still there, but ain't much of a Ranch left," Zeke said. "Another time twister just ran through it. I'm not sure it will ever be fixed. Looks like I'm going to have to find another way of doing the job."

"I believe in you," Finn said.

"Good to know I have the faith of another Foley," Zeke said. "Which is why I'm here. I made a promise to an old-timer—"

"Is he still in the Barn?" Finn interrupted.

"Nope. He's gone. It appears Time decided one Finn Foley was enough for this world. Anyway, he asked me to tell you something. I know where your father is hiding."

Finn gulped.

"When he told me, I had to laugh. All that technology he stole from the future, and it turns out the one thing he used was the most boring of the bunch. You saw a little of how it worked in the library of the domed city. Seems they had a gadget that stored information on a subatomic level," Zeke explained.

"You mean the STICKY?" Finn asked. He opened his palm and the translucent paper appeared. "It's still here! But if I changed everything, did I even go to the dome?"

"Technically, no, but you're going to need that thing to find your dad. Old Man Finn figured out a way to adapt that technology. He and his friends stored all kinds of stuff in the subatomic—food, weapons, and your father."

"Are you saying they shrank him?"

Zeke nodded. "Gimme your hand."

Finn did as he was asked. Zeke pressed the metal plates on his head. His eyes glowed and he turned Finn's hand over and over, examining both sides, as keenly as possible.

"There he is," the Ranger said, pointing under Finn's thumbnail. "Old Man Finn had him hidden in the pajamas. When you put them on, he was transferred to you. He's been with you the whole time."

Finn smiled and squinted at his thumb.

"So how do I get him back?"

"I wish I could help with that, but I'm not that smart. I suspect a clever kid like you will figure it out. You're a Foley. Thinking outside the box seems to be in your blood."

Zeke swung his lasso and created a new portal.

"Well, I better get to work. I let a few bad ones out of the Barn. They promised to be good, but I'm not going to take their word for it. Be kind to yourself, kid, and when you see your dad, tell him ol' Zeke says hello."

"I will," Finn promised.

"Oh, and, son, be careful," the Time Ranger warned as he stepped through the gateway. "This world ain't like the one you left behind."

"What do you mean?"

Zeke didn't answer, and a moment later he was gone.

"Finn!" his mother called to him from the kitchen window. She sounded panicked.

"Hey, Mom. How did you do on your test?"

She and Kate charged out of the house.

"How did you escape?" Mom threw her arms around him and burst into tears. Kate did the same.

"Escape what?"

"Get inside," she said. They practically dragged him through the back door and into the house. Once there, they turned off all the lights and locked the doors. Kate raced to the front window and closed the curtains. She poked her head through them to look out at the street.

"There's twenty of them out there, but I don't think they saw him," she said.

"Twenty who?" Finn asked. He walked over to pull the drapes open, but his mom yanked him back.

"Are you crazy? They'll come in here and take you away again. Oh, Finn, we've missed you so much. Did they hurt you?"

"Mom, I don't know what you're talking about," he said. He carefully peered outside, knowing that whatever was out there was making his mom and sister mental. One glance and he understood why. Marching down the street was a group of gigantic bugs—Plague soldiers, carrying enormous weapons on their shoulders. He could hear them clicking as they talked to one another.

"The bugs are back? When did that happen?" he asked.

"Honey? What are you talking about?" His mom pulled him away from the window. "Oh, they've done something to you, haven't they? Finn, the Plague never went away. They've been here since they conquered the planet."

"But we fought them back," he argued. "I stole their wormhole generator. I sent them to the farthest part of the universe. There's no way they could find their way back here."

"He's sick, Mom," Kate said. "They did something to him on the mother ship. No one ever comes back from there the same way."

Finn sat down in a chair, stunned, and then the truth hit him right in the gut.

"We didn't stop them, did we?" *There was never a "we"—no Lincoln. No Julep. The Plague took over the world because I never met my friends,* he said to himself.

"Come on!" Kate said, pulling him out of his seat. "We need to show you something."

They hurried him up the stairs into his old bedroom. It was just as he remembered it. His mom and Kate pushed his bed aside, then got on their hands and knees to pull up some loose floorboards. Once they were set aside, Mom reached into the darkness and came back out with a burlap sack. She shoved it into Finn's hands.

"Open it," she said.

Finn did as she had asked. Inside was a large silver object. When he took it out, he realized it was a robotic head with a glass screen for a face.

"Highbeam!" he exclaimed.

The icons on his digital face formed an exclamation point.

"Little man!"

"Where's the rest of your body?" Finn asked.

An arrow pointing upward appeared on Highbeam's face.

"The bugs have it. How did you escape?"

"Listen, everyone, I need to tell you something, but it's going to be hard to believe," Finn said. "Though it shouldn't, when you think about everything we've gone through. It's a long story and I'll do the best I can to explain it, but this wasn't supposed to happen."

"This?" Kate asked.

"Everything. The bugs didn't conquer Earth. They aren't in the streets right now. I'm not in a prison on the mother ship. None of this happened."

"I'm sorry, kid. It's hard on all of us, but the facts are the facts. Listen, I'm happy to see you, but you should never have come back here. The whole armada will be looking for you. This is the first place they'll come."

"Wait!" Finn lifted his shirt. The familiar and strange alien technology was fused to his chest again. "It's back! The wormhole generator is back! Where's the lunchbox?"

Kate reached into the sack that held Highbeam's head and pulled out a very pink, very rainbow-covered sparkly unicorn lunchbox.

"We kept it hidden. The bugs couldn't get their creepy hands on it, too," she said.

"Okay, this is excellent news. So, where is Pre'at?" Finn asked.

"Pre'at?" Highbeam said. "She's locked up on the mother ship, where you're supposed to be!"

"We're going to rescue them," Finn explained.

"Are you nuts? You just escaped!" Kate cried.

Finn turned to his mother.

"And then we're going to find Dad. I know where he is, Mom, and when we find him, he can change everything back to the way it is supposed to be!"

"I think you caught space cooties or something," Kate said to him.

"Trust me. I'm going to make everything right, just like I did the first time. The only thing I need are my two best friends in the world, Lincoln Sidana and Julep Li."

TO BE CONCLUDED . . .

The Thank-Yous

Lots of people help make a book. Some do it directly, while others have no idea what they've contributed. To the strangers on the train, the kids at schools all over the country, and many a long-lost friend, thank you for the inspiration.

The folks who made the biggest difference to this series deserve a special shout-out: my editor, Wendy Loggia, who smiles so big when we talk about these books (I know you told me not to write a time-travel story—I'll listen next time); the team at Delacorte Press, who renewed my faith in what I do with their enthusiasm; my agent, Alison Fargis, and her team at Stonesong, for listening to my bizarre ideas with straight faces; my son, Finn, who inspired all the jokes and acts of heroism; Kirsten Miller, for endless inspiration, laughter, and tacos; and Joe Deasy and Mark Kilian for listening.

I couldn't have done it without you.

IT ALL BEGINS IN . . .

A strange, blinking device is stuck on Finn Foley . . . and a group of gigantic bugs want it back. They'll stop at nothing to get it—even if it means destroying the world.

About the Author

Michael Buckley lives in a part of New York known for evil robot attacks. Luckily, his son, Finn, and their magical wonder dog, Friday, are at his side. Together, they defend the peaceful and simple people of Brooklyn from the metallic, brain-eating horde. Somehow, during all the fires and chaos, Michael found time to write twenty books. They include the Sisters Grimm series and the NERDS series. You might like them. A lot of people suffered while he wrote them. It was time he should have dedicated to fighting the robots.

Do you have more questions? Do you have tips on fighting evil robots? Take a peek at michaelbuckley writes.com, his weird videos on YouTube, and his Instagram page at @buckleystopshere.